ALSO BY CAESAR RONDINA
A Woman's Fear
The Warrior Within
Life Through A Mirror
Making Partnership Choices
Balancing The Scale
Who Are The Heroes
The Soul In Our Hearts
Best Selling Author of
Management and Employee Relations
(available as a tutorial on udemy.com)
Leadership Skills for Success

www.caesarrondinaauthor.com Twitter - @
caesarrondina Facebook - Caesar Rondina Author

All names and events in this book are fictional
and do not relate to any people or events.

FROM BEST SELLING AUTHOR
CAESAR RONDINA

LIFE
THROUGH
A
MIRROR

THE BATTLE RAGES ON

authorHOUSE®

AuthorHouse™
1663 Liberty Drive
Bloomington, IN 47403
www.authorhouse.com
Phone: 1 (800) 839-8640

Published by AuthorHouse 12/10/2018

ISBN: 978-1-5462-7183-3 (sc)
ISBN: 978-1-5462-7181-9 (hc)
ISBN: 978-1-5462-7182-6 (e)

Library of Congress Control Number: 2018914648

Print information available on the last page.

Any people depicted in stock imagery provided by Getty Images are models, and such images are being used for illustrative purposes only. Certain stock imagery © Getty Images.

This book is printed on acid-free paper.

CONTENTS

DEDICATION

This book is dedicated to my family who has supported me throughout my journey and to every individual who enjoys a good murder mystery. I appreciate every reader, not just the ones that follow me, but all readers. Your dedication keeps a wonderful form of creativity, expression, and art alive. I would like to thank all those who have supported me along this path.

INTRODUCTION

In the first book of the continuing murder mystery series, *"Life through a Mirror,"* you met individuals who had a great influence on Allie and David. Their past, present, and what might be their future. Allie and David had never met. Eventually, they would meet during their quest to fix their past and clear their names. As the plot developed, strong family bonds were developed. Challenges arose that almost destroyed their family and relationship. Allie came from a small New England town. She had a past. Prostitution and stealing were all she knew. She needed to survive. She was charged and convicted of manslaughter and served ten years in prison.

David also came from a New England town. He was raised two towns over from Allie. It was a much larger town. Growing up, they never met. After college, he took a job in New York as a criminal defense attorney. David and his best friend Paulie attended many parties and had many women. They fell into a trap set by a crime family. They fell prey to money, cars, drugs, drinking, women, and gambling. Debts always need to be paid. Nothing comes free. The result from these actions would lead to David losing his job and ability to practice law in that region. He lost it all. Paulie also lost his job, and slowly became more involved in the crime family. Allie and David were stuck in a tangled web. A silky web spun by many spiders to catch their prey. Allie and David would have to fight harder than before to break free of this web. A web that could destroy their family and everything they have achieved.

Will David and Allie go back to what they were? Will there be other options? Many times, people are forced into situations. It will take cunning as well as the ability to stick together to escape the web strung by the spiders in the second in the "life Through A Mirror, The Battle Rages On" murder mystery series. As you read *"Life Through A Mirror, The Battle Rages On,"* you will find at times, trouble follows people. Would trouble follow David and Allie? The truth can be bent, twisted, and made to appear like anything other than the truth. Will the truth be revealed as Allie and David have their past continue to haunt them and face new challenges and murder? Murder never comes neatly wrapped in a box and a pretty bow.

CHAPTER 1

LOOKING BACK

When we left off, Allie was six months pregnant with their son. Their home was a grand addition to the main family house. Except for the landscaping and driveway, the house was completed. Molly, David's mother, went with Allie to buy furniture for the house. Allie's case was overturned, and all references and charges regarding her murder conviction were removed from her record. She was cleared, and the charges were dropped for the murder of Carol, who she was later accused of killing. David had received his privileges to practice law in New York and received his privileges in Vermont where he now resided. His father, Lou, asked him to join his law firm as a full partner. They planned to establish a criminal-defense branch of the firm. Lou had never taken the firm to that level because he hoped that David would return home one day and become a partner at the firm. Lou's dream came true. David was now home to stay. One day, it would all belong to David. The firm and assets were worth millions. With the publicity from Allie's cases, David was now the most sought-after criminal defense attorney in the region. Business could not have been better. Allie, David, Molly, and Lou, developed a stronger family bond and friendship. Together, they passed the most difficult tests during those difficult times.

Lou was a quiet man and very intelligent. He did not give his opinion that often, but when he did, everyone listened. His demeanor alone commanded respect. Lou was instrumental in developing the town and its continuing growth. The town offered something for every season. Hunting, skiing, camping, boating, and fishing were available to the local resident and tourists. It boasted pristine woods and lakes. Lou knew how to capitalize on this. The town was one of the most sought-after vacation spots in New England. The town was always clean. Not a piece of paper was found in the street. The town had the best of everything while keeping its quaint country-style appearance and atmosphere. There were no serious crimes. Their laws were strict, and an experienced police force was on hand to handle anything that might occur. Unlike most other areas and towns, this town did not have to rely on the seasonal tourist. It attracted tourists year round.

The layout of the town was excellent for tourists. The town was modernized while keeping its quaint country-style appearance. This downtown area was zoned as the "Historic District" to preserve its heritage. It remained separated from the outskirts of town. The larger malls, dance bars, fast-food restaurants, and other businesses were located away from the historic district on the roads leading into and out of the downtown area. It was a fifteen-minute drive to reach the outside of town, which was located close to the newly built highway. Access to the highway was ideal. The highway was the main reason the town grew so quickly. The town council never wanted the historic district to lose its appeal for those that made it their permanent home. The town council wanted the historic district to be far enough from the outlying areas to keep the different lifestyles separate. That was paramount to everyone who resided there as the town grew. There were dances on Saturday nights and festivities on the holidays. The town was similar to a closely-knit family. All were welcome, and it maintained its family appeal. The shops in the center of town closed at six o'clock except for two restaurants and a pharmacy. The downtown businesses were owned by the residents and catered to the tourist trade. The downtown area offered a variety of businesses. Craft shops, dress shops, a hardware store, bed and breakfast establishments, an old-fashioned general store and fully remodeled hotel, as well as others. Maintaining a family atmosphere was paramount in this part of town. During the week, the two main restaurants in town stayed open until nine in the evening and ten o'clock on the weekends. When the workday was over, it was family time. The businesses on the main roads leading into and out of the town stayed followed their own set hours. Combined, the bed and breakfast lodgings in town and the hotel were booked all year, and the lodging establishments on the outskirts of town enjoyed the same success. Many enjoyed the old town family atmosphere, while others enjoyed the more modern style of the nightclubs, bars, and other attractions outside of town. The hotels and motels outside of town had few vacancies due to the overflow from the main town. Friends stopped over to visit other friends at night. "The Café," was a less formal restaurant, whereas "The Tavern," was a more elegant restaurant. On the weekend, unless you were a regular or had a reservation, you had no chance of getting into either restaurant during the busy dinner hours. They would leave some tables open for the locals that were there weekly. Both restaurants were large and had ample seating capacity.

Molly, David's mother, owned a specialty dress shop in town that catered to both the middle and high-end buyer. She sold a full line of women's accessories as well. Molly, a beautiful woman, carried herself with grace and was a down-to-earth person. Molly looked upon Allie as a daughter. Molly's daughter Jessica was killed by a drunk driver when she was eight years old. Molly's love and devotion to David had no boundaries. She felt sad that her daughter would not be part of her life and business, especially now, that David was partners with her husband, Lou. For Molly, Allie took Jessica's place. Allie loved fashion. Allie chose to enter into a partnership with Molly and expand the shop to include a day spa and hair salon. Allie created her designer clothing line called Allie M. With everyone's past now behind them. These were exciting times. Almost six months had passed since everything had been resolved, and life appeared to be back to normal. Allie was due in three weeks. Her wedding plans with David's were to take place in two months. Allie and David did not want to wait long before Allie got pregnant again. They were getting older and wanted their children to be close in age. They were hoping for a girl the next time. Could life be any better? Getting to this point in their lives was hard work. Allie was unknown in the fashion industry but had great patterns and sketches of her work. Once the line was in production, Allie hoped that being close to some large retail stores, along with the tourist trade would help her brand to become recognized.

It was found out later that Logan Miller murdered the town council member Jack. Allie did not commit the murder as previously thought. This finding was instrumental in getting Allie's murder conviction overturned. It was determined that Jack's murder was orchestrated by Tom, the town sheriff, and the "Judge," who were both from the town where Allie previously lived. The sheriff's girlfriend Carol also played an instrumental part in these events. The "Judge." opened up many new cases for the FBI. He was nicknamed the "Judge" because he was also the town judge at the time. He ultimately turned on everyone and became a witness for the FBI. In turn for his information and testimony, he and his family would enter the witness protection program. As a group, they were referred to them as the "Crew." Carol was killed during a struggle with Allie and Allie was arrested for her murder. No evidence could be found to prove Allie's claim of self -defense. The "Crew" was a dirty bunch. They lined their pockets while the town people struggled to survive. They built a barn outside of town many years back. Although it looked like an average barn from the outside, inside, there was a large room for gambling, rooms for prostitution, and it served as a major hub for drug trafficking and weapons in and out of New England region. As the case unfolded, it was found that many who were involved were individuals the FBI had been trying to arrest for years. In most of these cases, obtaining evidence was difficult. Russell was the investigator Lou, and David hired. He was instrumental in finding out that the "Barn" was built on land owned by the federal government. The FBI could now enter the case. Not even the town was aware of since it had been located there for years.

Lou had known Russel from when he was born. Lou was friends with Russel's father for years. While Russel was growing up, he learned the investigation business from his father who was a retired agent for the CIA. He went to college and became a partner in his father's investigation firm after graduation. Russell was instrumental in getting the company known globally. Lou used their services on many occasions regarding other cases. Russell's father had many connections. He was forced to retire due to an illness. Lou was a supportive friend during his recovery. Russell took the lead in the investigation on Allie and David's past. His work was instrumental in obtaining the information they needed to have their names cleared, and resulted in the arrests of many other crime figures from New York, Florida, and Vermont. These turn of events were a big break for Ray, the prosecutor. Ray would find out all the things he needed to build a solid case against the crime bosses the FBI had been tracking for years. It would take months to put this information together. The crime families hired many attorneys. These cases were rock solid, and timing would be a key factor.

Allie and David knew they may be required to be involved in these future cases. They choose not to think about this during this time. David and Paulie were best friends. They grew up together. Paulie moved to New York when David did. After David was used as a pawn, he left the city after losing his privileges and his job. Paulie stayed at the city and was now working his way up the ladder within the crime family. Paulie loved this lifestyle. He enjoyed feeling important wherever he went. Pauline was instrumental in assisting Russel by obtaining the vital information required to clear David. Although David did not approve of his lifestyle, they were best friends since childhood. Without Paulie, David and Allie might not be where they were today. He would never forget what Paulie did for him. However, they had an unspoken understanding. At times, no words are necessary between friends. They just know. David would see Paulie from when he came to town to visit his mom and dad. They owned a craft shop in town. David and Paulie were inseparable as friends. They grew up in the same town. Both were high school football stars and popular among women. It is not surprising that Paulie being in the big city would get involved with this crowd. Paulie was involved with this crowd due to Davis involved. An involvement he thought was innocent at the time.

David and Allie clicked. They had a connection. David was very athletic and always stayed in shape. Allie was breathtaking. Her beautiful long blonde hair accented her features well. She was perfect in every way. She could easily be a top model. While in prison, a woman who liked Allie felt bad for her. She helped her to learn much about life and helped Allie to focus and take the correct path. Many nights while lying in bed next to Allie, he would think of how lucky he was. He also knew as much as their past was behind

5

them, this was not over. He had a bad feeling. In a sense, David was much like Lou. He could remove his emotions from an equation and examine the facts. It assisted him to form his initial decision. Later, he would account for the emotional factors. David and Allie were very much in love. In their own way, they helped to save one another. A strong bond developed between them. Even though Lou and Molly were parental figures, they were also great friends. Allie and David were strong individuals. She did not take any crap. That is what kept David in check. However, David was a more rational person than Allie was. That is what kept her in check. Overall, next to Molly and Lou, they were a great team. As wealthy as the family was, they acted like everyday people. They were down to earth and worked hard for what they had. Nothing was handed to them. They appreciated this and gave a great deal back to the community. They cooked meals at home, went to the town's festivities, dances, and attended church each week. At times, they would stay in town to have dinner when Lou and David worked late. They might eat at the local pizza restaurant, "The Tavern" or "The Café." They did enjoy one special night out as a family each week, or with friends. As good as things were, none of them forgot what got them there. The hardest part came when Allie and David were apart. The family constantly argued. The family was torn and divided. After getting through these times, they all made a promise. They would never allow this to happen again.

Carol was killed during her altercation with Allie. Allie insisted it was in self-defense. The police could not find any other weapons or evidence to support her claim. This led to the arrest of Allie for Carol's murder. It would be difficult at best, to prove self-defense. The strain was unbearable. While awaiting trial, Allie discovered she was pregnant. This while having to face the possibility of spending the rest of her life in prison, was overwhelming. Due to the lack of evidence to back Allie's claim, Molly and Lou were starting to have their doubts. David and his parents began fighting. In time, David was starting to question Allie's story. Russell sat with the family and pulled them together by reminding them of all they had been through as a family and survived. His firm but gentle demeanor was what they needed that renewed their faith in each other, and strengthened their family bond. The truth eventually was found. Truth is a funny thing. If you never stop looking for it, you may find it in the strangest places. Without Russel, this would have been a broken family, and Allie could be spending the rest of her life in prison. Every card in the deck was stacked against her. There was a lack of evidence, motive, a history of conflicts between Carol and Allie, a previous murder conviction, and only the word of Allie. The only other witness was Carol, as she was dead. The evidence they had was more than enough for any prosecutor to make a clean case and get a conviction. Once again, Allie was fighting the battle of her life. A battle she felt she was losing.

In the end, as many things began to surface, the facts led to many arrests, with more to come. At times, it seems that when life is going well, something comes along to bend the path. The crime families that the FBI would be going after were not small organizations. The bosses covered their tracks quite well. How else could they avoid arrests and convictions for all these years? Because they always used an intermediary, it was hard to catch them dirty. They trusted very few people. Rewarding the loyal ones, and punishing those that betrayed them. Times were different than they were in past years. Technology had advanced, and the ability to obtain information was more efficient. The old-school loyalty was changing within this modern time crime element. The older fears disappeared with many being offered the witness protection program. If arrested, everyone was out for number one. The witness protection program made it easier for law enforcement officers to get criminals to roll over on one another. Times certainly changed. Getting into the program was not easy. A person had to provide valuable information to be considered for the program. It had to lead to an arrest and conviction. They would also have to be willing to testify. Due to prison overcrowding, the modern-day legal system had become one plea bargain after another. Law enforcement did whatever it took to chip away at these crime figures with the hopes of getting the larger players. Drones, surveillance systems, and other means of technology were used. The crime families had to be much more careful. It was no longer the days of murders and gun battles in the streets. It was all about business and making money. What was good for business was good for the organization. Everyone from the bottom up had to pay up the ladder. They had to hustle for them to make a buck. If they did, they were well off and reaped the benefits. If they did not, they did not last long. The case that Ray would bring to trial would be landmark cases, arrests, and convictions. If he were successful, his career would skyrocket.

David lost his privileges because the prosecuting attorney in New York suspected he took part in a conspiracy to get a notebook in evidence, removed from the evidence room. This notebook contained crucial information and would lead to the conviction of the largest crime boss in New York and others that were involved with racketeering, prostitution, drugs and more. Without the notebook, the prosecutor did not have a case. At the time, the prosecutor for the city had a political agenda. A conviction would make it all happen. The notebook went missing from the evidence room a few days before the trial leaving the prosecutor with no hard evidence. The case would be dismissed. These events made the prosecutor come under scrutiny and look like a complete idiot. It ruined any chance at his political career. Since David and Paulie were foolish enough to get themselves involved with this criminal element, the prosecutor believed that David and Paulie were involved in some way. The prosecutor could not prove beyond all doubts they were involved. Therefore, he could not arrest them and press charges against them. He was going to use any meaning available to ruin them.

He had Paulie fired from his job, and Paulie began to become more involved in the crime family. He also used whatever political connections he had left to get David disbarred. He was relentless until he succeeded to destroy David's name and reputation. David's firm fired him. David could not get a job that paid anything substantial anywhere in the city. He was also at a turning point in his life. David was also addicted to drugs. Sharon, a drug counselor he represented in a case, came to his aid. She helped him to beat his addiction. Without her help, David's life might have been destroyed. He had to change his ways. He loved to party, drink, do drugs, gamble, and especially loved women. When his parents heard of this, they would be devastated. He had to figure this out and find a way to clear his name and start over. Time was against him. He thought it was better his family heard this from him, rather than through other sources.

8

With nothing left to his name but his car and clothes, he went back home to talk with his family. It had been two years since he was there. Thanksgiving was approaching, which would be a good reason for David to go home for a visit. At least, his family would be happy he was visiting. For David, there was nowhere else to turn. He had to begin a new life.

The spine-tingling details of all these events could be found in the first of this series, *"Life Through A Mirror."* Now for the continuing saga of;

"Life Through A Mirror"
"The Battle Rages On."

CHAPTER 2

THE PRESENT DAY

It was a Sunday morning. Allie, David, Molly, and Lou were having breakfast. Allie was experiencing false labor for the past few days. Her pregnancy was normal, and the baby was fine. She was due any day. Allie reached a point that she could not wait for this to be over. The baby's room was finished and decorated. While everyone was getting ready for church, Allie started to experience contractions. They felt the same as the previous times. She thought this was also false labor. Lately, everyone has been busy. The store expansion for Molly and Allie was a great success. In addition to the clothing store, they now offered hair styling, a day spa, massages, and more. Business could not be better. All the work involved with completing the expansion and starting up the Allie M. designer clothing line was tiring for Allie. However, she refused to slow down. Allie was always moving in high gear. The contractions subsided, and the family left for church. The people in town looked upon the church as a spiritual experience, but also a way to stay in touch. After the last mass each week, there was brunch. Everyone was welcome. The women in the parish would take weekly turns doing the cooking. Anyone who was also available would also pitch in to help. It was a great way for the townspeople to spend time together.

During mass, Allie's contractions returned. This time they were different. They were much stronger, and her water broke. Allie was in excellent shape before her pregnancy and remained active throughout her pregnancy. She modified her exercise routine as her mobility changed. She leaned over and said to David, "I think it's time babe. My water broke." As Allie got closer to her due date, they took an overnight bag with them everywhere they went. David leaned over to Lou to let him know. Of course, the expecting grandparents were much less calm than Allie and David. Allie's contractions were still far apart and were lasting 30 to 45 seconds. There was plenty of time to get her to the hospital since it was only ten minutes away. Lou, being the proud grandfather, interrupted mass and excused the family. Everyone wished them well as they left for the hospital. With all that Allie and David had been through over the past months, the town was behind them and very supportive. They were equally excited for Allie and David. On the way to the hospital, David explained they should have taken two cars in the event Lou and Molly wanted to leave. There was no telling how long Allie would be in labor. Lou and Molly laughed. There was no way Allie or David could talk them into leaving. Lou pulled up to the front of the hospital, and David went inside and explained the situation. A nurse came out with a wheelchair. Allie and David went inside as Molly and Lou followed. The valet attendant parked their car. Once the nurse signed Allie in, they brought her directly to labor and delivery.

The nurse had everyone except David wait outside the room while Allie change. The resident doctor came in to examine her. After letting the family in, he explained she still had some time to go. Allie elected to have an epidural when the time came. The staff notified her private doctor when she arrived. David asked Paulie to be the Godfather. He called him to let him know Allie would be having the baby. Paulie was very excited to hear this news and told David he would be there tomorrow, and to call him if anything changed. About an hour later, there was a flower delivery to the room. They were from Paulie. Everyone was supportive of Allie during her labor. Allie would not let Molly leave her side. At one-point, Allie started to cry. Allie felt bad that her mother disowned her many years back while she was in prison. She moved away and never had further contact with her. She never let Allie know where she relocated. Part of Allie wished she could be there. Another part of her had no use for her. As Allie's life changed, due to her anger towards her mother, she never missed her. Deep inside, she always hoped they could see one another one day, but she never tried to find her. Allie explained her tears to everyone.

Molly and Lou asked, "Allie, do you want us to try to find her and let her know?"

Allie replied, "No." Allie felt that if her mother cared enough about her, she would have tried to contact her by now. Allie's case was all over the news. Finding her would not be difficult if someone wanted to.

Allie explained to everyone, "You all are my family now."

Lou wanted to change the subject. He laughed and asked, "Are you still naming this angel after me?"

At the same time, Allie and David both replied, "Are you kidding? He will be Louis David Romano." Lou could not hold back his tears of joy.

Molly said, "Let's get this show on the road. You have to start working on my granddaughter. You're not getting off that easy." Everyone laughed.

About three hours had passed. Molly and Lou were going to the cafeteria to get some food. As they stood up, the priest from church arrived with a huge plate of salads and sandwiches from the earlier brunch.

David asked, "Father, are you planning on feeding an army?"

The priest replied, "This is from all the people in town, and they wanted to send their best wishes. Everyone wants to know how you are doing."

He sat with them for a short time, and they said a prayer together. He blessed the family and left. Allie's contractions were coming much closer now and lasting longer. Her private doctor came in and asked everyone to leave for a moment so she could examine Allie. By this time, Allie felt she was ready for the epidural. Her doctor agreed it was time. Allie was now much closer to delivering. The doctor called for the team to administer the epidural. She wanted to know who Allie wanted to be in the room with her when she gave birth. Allie replied, "All my family please."

The doctor told her that was fine. Everything was going well. The baby was in the correct position. Allie did well with the pain. Her doctor did not expect the epidural to slow the process down by much since she waited so long. The team came in and administered the epidural. Allie felt more comfortable, but it still hurt. The doctor left and explained she would be back to check on her. She told Allie if anything changes, she was to push the call button immediately. The nurse was in often to check on her.

Soon the contractions got stronger. Allie started to feel as if she needed to push. "I think it's time," Allie said. As soon as she hit the call button, the doctor and nurse came right in.

The doctor took one look and said, "Honey. It's time to have this baby."

Molly and Lou stepped off to the side. David stayed right by Allie's side, coaching her every step of the way. The birthing process was well underway. With coaching and some pushing, her baby boy was born. It was a normal delivery. The baby was beautiful. David had to privilege to cut the cord then the doctor wrapped the baby and handed him to Allie. After a moment passed, the nurse took him. They needed to clean and check him. When that process was completed, the family would get to spend time with the baby. Allie still had the remainder of the birthing process to complete. It was around three o'clock in the morning. The baby weighed eight pounds and four ounces. The pediatrician checked the baby, and the nurses cleaned him. Allie and the family could hold him again. It was a joyful moment for everyone. A day in Allie's life she thought would never come. Her road was long and hard and filled with many obstacles. Everyone had an opportunity to hold the baby. The remainder of the birthing process went smoothly. Many of the town people lived outside of town, which encompassed a wide geographical area. The town used a call tree system for emergencies or special announcements. In no time, the entire town received the news that David and Allie had their baby. As excited as Allie was, she was exhausted. It was time for the baby to go into the nursery, and Allie needed to get some rest. She tore more than expected and was uncomfortable.

David wanted to stay the night with Allie. The nurse said that was fine and brought in a recliner and some blankets for David. The owner of the hotel in town had already called Lou and told him to come over when he was ready. They had a room all set up for Lou and Molly so they would not have to drive all the way home. They wanted to stay, but the hospital would not allow that many people to sleep in the room. The room was not big enough, and Allie needed her rest. Molly and Lou left for the hotel. It did not take long for Allie and David to fall asleep. David did not sleep in the recliner. He cuddled next to Allie in the bed to hold her, and they both fell asleep. When the nurse came in, she did not have the heart to wake them. Everyone knew the following day would bring many visitors, and Paulie was coming as well. After all, he was going to be the baby's Godfather. Allie became good friends with the daughter of another shop owner. Her name was Julie. She was Paulie's sister. She planned to ask her to be the baby's Godmother but never got around to it. She worked in the spa which Allie and Molly were now partners. She was their manager and well as a hair stylist. Allie and Julie were the same age. Julie just became engaged to a very nice man from town. They planned to get together when Paulie came to town. Allie thought she would ask Julie at that time. Paulie did not come home to visit his family as often as he would like to, or should.

It was early summer. The landscaping and driveway to the new house were completed. Everything fell into place nicely and as planned. Allie and David had their wedding coming up in two months. Allie was the type that was able to lose weight quickly. She was not a big eater and worked out daily. She was not concerned about losing the extra weight before she had to slip into her wedding gown. Molly and Allie had had a small room in the back of the shop so Allie could bring the baby to work each day rather than place him in daycare right away. Allie was anxious to get back to work. Before Allie came to town, Molly worked in her shop with one part-time high school girl who worked after school and on weekends. With the new addition of the spa, the business grew rapidly gaining many new clients. Allie and Molly were busy designing their clothing line and buying for the shop. They increased their staff to five other employees plus a manager. After Lou and Molly's daughter died, Lou made the back parking lot at the complex very safe. It had a full-time security guard, a daycare center, and a playground for the children. Those who had children or worked in town were never far from their children. This was an ideal situation for anyone with children that worked in town.

*****

Later that day Paulie arrived. His face lit up with joy upon seeing the baby that would soon be his Godson and brought many gifts. Paulie was also Italian. He followed the customs of his heritage. He and Julie came to visit Allie and the baby at the hospital. Allie could not wait until they all were together. She wanted to ask Julie to be the baby's Godmother. When Allie asked her, Julie was excited that Allie considered her and gladly accepted. Allie had many visitors that day. The family had spread the word asking people to wait for Allie to come home to visit so she could rest. After two days, Allie was able to take the baby home. Other people from the town came to visit, bringing food, and other items to the house. Molly, Lou, and Julie were already planning the christening and party. The church hall would be perfect for this occasion. Anyone who wanted to come would be welcome. Lou would not need to cater the event. Everyone from town would cook and bring food. It was a town tradition. No matter how much this town grew, this area kept their traditions and heritage.

Paulie, Julie, and his family were over the house for dinner a couple of days after Allie came home from the hospital. Paulie told David before he left town he needed to speak with him. David told him of course. Paulie explained tonight was not the time or place. They made plans to meet the following day. At one time, Paulie and David were both associated with the same crime family. In David's case, they were clients of the law firm who employed him. Paulie was along for the ride. Not knowing what Paulie needed to discuss, he would never forget that Paulie was the lynchpin that saved his career. David would always feel like he owed Paulie. As best friends, they always said, "We never owe one another, it's what we do." David was not going to try to imagine what this was all about, but he was sure it had something to do with Paulie's involvement with the crime family. David already helped Vincent, the head of the family, once. That was what caused him to be disbarred. He decided not to think about it and enjoy the evening. He would find out soon enough. Earlier that day he received a voice message from Ray, the federal prosecutor who was involved with taking down the "Crew." Ray wanted to let David know that all the information provided by the "Judge" would lead to many other arrests and convictions that could take down one of the largest drug trafficking rings on the east coast. They were almost ready to put all this information together along with everyone's findings.

David returned Ray's call earlier, but it went to his voicemail. He apologized for the delay getting back to him and explained that Allie had the baby. He did not hear back from Ray as of yet. David had a feeling that Ray's call, and what Paulie needed to speak to him about, would be somehow related. David, Allie, Russ, and Lou, agreed to work with Ray if needed when these other cases come up. After everyone left, Molly and Allie were cleaning up and checking on the baby. David told Lou about Paulie's request. Lou was a bit concerned. He knew Paulie would only want to speak with David. Due to their history and involvement with these people, Lou wanted to be in the loop.

Lou said, "Son, you came back from hell, and turned it into heaven. Do not get caught up in this again. Let's communicate on this."

David replied, "Don't worry dad. I did not come back from hell alone. You helped get me out of my mess and turn it into heaven. We are a family and a team. Nothing will ever jeopardize that again."

David had plans to meet Paulie at eleven in the morning. When the "Judge" made the deal to roll over and enter the witness protection program, Ray knew it would take months to put all these cases and indictments together. The biggest challenge would be to make all these arrests at the same time. Confiscate all they could, and try to bundle it all together. There were many players between drug trafficking, prostitution, and racketeering. If any of this got out, if even one boss were to get arrested before another, that would give the others time to cover their tracks.

Ray was very fortunate that the raid on the barn produced many videotapes. These recording identified many people in compromising positions. Many of the recorded transactions included sexual acts for money and gambling. These facts placed many of these crime bosses right in the thick of it, including drugs and weapons. The "Judge," he had the real dirt. The "Judge knew a great deal about the organization. He knew how the money was laundered, where it went, and who received it. He also knew which holding and shell companies they used, and the bank account numbers. He knew who was involved in other unsolved murders, and where most of the records were kept. Tom, the sheriff and ringleader of the "Crew," liked to brag and talk. It made him feel important. Tom had all the dirt on these people. He looked at it as an insurance policy. Let's call it protection. However, Tom was a minor player in a much bigger game. A game he did not know how to play. The fact that he liked to brag is what made him so vulnerable and easy to catch. Tom was a show-off. Being he was the town sheriff, he thought he was untouchable. Everyone was amazed that due to one girl named Allie, who was trying to get her name cleared, resulted in all these other criminal activities that surfaced. With the help of David, his family, and Russell, this turned out to be one hell of a catch. Ray developed a task force solely for this. He handpicked the agents who would be involved. He knew he would only get one chance to take them all down at the same time. He was still in the process of putting some missing pieces together. If successful, this would be the ticket to his political career and further aspirations. He was determined not to lose this opportunity.

The following morning, Ray returned David's call. David thanked him for the flowers he sent to Allie as they began to talk. With everything that took place in the past, they had all become very close and good friends. At the time, Lou was in David's office. They placed the call on speakerphone. After hearing the details of the baby, Ray started the conversation. He explained that they had checked and rechecked all the investigative work. They had gone over everything many times. The best agents were working on these cases. Ray went on to explain that they had accumulated a great deal of evidence and testimony, including phone records, financials, and the videos. They also discovered the identity of the person from the blood discovered in the barn. The "Judge," along with the other evidence we had in place, helped to tie this all together. The "Judge" also informed us where to find the body of the murdered victim. They buried it a hole dug in the woods.

Ray said, "Dave, I am ready to take down the heads of three major crime families."

David replied, "You know these people cover their tracks and often do things through others. Are you expecting more people to roll over?"

Ray admitted, "Yes. I am sure I will need a couple of people to become witnesses for the government. We will get them into the program. This way, we can tie up any loose ends. We may need additional information to prove direct contact and who gave the orders. I'm confident for reasons I can't discuss, I can make that happen."

David and Lou thought this was great news. Ray explained, "As we make this happen, you know I might need Allie to confirm some of the things she saw. If that is needed, I will certainly try to keep her out of it as much as I can, but it may be necessary."

"I know," David replied. "We have spoken about this and knew this day might come. I appreciate that you will try to keep it to a minimum, especially now with the baby being here."

Ray said, "I'll do my best." He went on to say, "It was a month or so before this would come together, and it would take months before all the trials would go to court." David explained he would assist in any legal way he could.

Ray said, "I would love to have you in on this, but you're not a federal employee. I appreciate your offer to help, and I am happy that I can discuss things with you."

Ray told them he would be in touch and let him know what was going on. David thanked him, and they ended their call.

Lou and David were quite impressed by this information. Knowing Ray, they did not expect anything less. They discussed it for a while and then there was silence. They looked at each other and knew what they were thinking. What they had thought was the end, was only going to be the beginning. They had a good idea what Paulie wanted to discuss with David. David had one quick case in court for a simple traffic matter before he met with Paulie. He wrapped that up and met Paulie on time at the diner as agreed. Paulie did not seem to be himself. He looked very serious. Once David heard what he had to say, he would know why. Paulie started from the bottom in the crime family. He had to pay his dues, but he loved the lifestyle. Paulie was ambitious. It did not take him long to work his way up in the organization. He was at a level where he had his own small territory and people under him. He was no longer a grunt. However, Paulie was not high enough up the ladder to have intimate knowledge on most things. Vincent knew of everyone in his organization and kept his distance. He rarely associated with those at the lower end of the food chain, although the expectations to perform were always there. There were many levels to climb before anyone came close to the man at the top. To those below you, you were the king. Your word was the law. Everyone had expectations and expected them to be carried out. The person above you did not care if the captain made money. They had a price they had to pay up to the boss, no matter what. Taking care of business was their problem. The rewards were great, but the demand was high. Anything short of total loyalty was unacceptable.

After talking about the baby, David asked Paulie what was wrong. Paulie started to tell David that Vincent, the big boss, heard rumors he would be under investigation again. Being investigated had become routine. With everything that had taken place, Paulie did not know if it was related to these new findings or older matters. However, this time Vincent heard that the FBI was involved. Paulie could only assume it had something to do with the recent investigations regarding the "Barn." Paulie did not know if Vincent ever had any dealings with the people from the "Barn." He only knew that Vincent liked David from when he used to represent him when he worked for the firm in New York. It came down the pipeline that Vincent wanted Paulie to ask David to be part of his defense team. Vincent was not happy with the lawyers the firm used to replace David.

Paulie said, "If this is true, I know this would put you in a very difficult position, especially if it had something to do with the FBI task force that Ray had developed." That is not a secret.

Paulie knew that Ray helped David as much as David helped him. There were many unknowns. Even though David used to hang out with that crowd, and represented many of them through his old firm, David felt he owed them nothing. He did what he had to do for whatever reasons in the past. No obligations existed. No favors were owed. After Allie's case, David's reputation was incredible. Vincent wanted to retain him. By reaching out through Paulie, Vincent felt David would become part of his legal team out of his friendship with Paulie.

In the past, when all of this came to a head and Allie was acquitted, their FBI agreement only pertained to being available for information sharing and any testimony they might need from Allie or Russell regarding findings, or what was seen or heard. There was never any mention of David having the ability to represent anyone if contacted. David's concern was if he took Vincent's case, it could be viewed as a conflict of interest, especially if it had anything to do with the past findings from previous cases where he was the defense attorney and had information that could affect the prosecutor's case. At this point, David did not know what Vincent's charges would be. There were many unknowns, and this could become very complicated. On the other hand, David had concerns as to how this could affect Paulie in the organization. If David refused, would that jeopardize Paulie? David told Paulie they had to bring Lou in on this. They both knew what could be at stake. Paulie agreed. Now that David knew, Paulie knew he would tell Lou. They set up a time the following night to discuss this together. Everyone would come to the house and have dinner. The girls could play with the baby and chat, while he and Paulie talked with Lou. When they were done, David returned to the office and went directly to Lou's office to make him aware of the conversation.

Lou replied, "Well. We did not figure on this. This is going to be a very difficult decision that will require some thought."

David said, "I could always talk to Vincent and find out what this is all about, and still have the option to decline. It would need to be carefully orchestrated."

They both knew Paulie needed an answer. David could not help but wonder. Was he helping Vincent or Paulie? David didn't care about Vincent. However, he did care about Paulie. Could there be ramifications if he said no? They would know more after they spoke with Paulie later that night.

It was a busy day at the office. Lou and David did not have any time to discuss it further. Molly and Allie were also having a busy day. Molly called Lou at the end of the day and asked if he minded eating in town. She and Allie were exhausted from the day and did not feel like cooking. David and Lou were tired as well and thought that was a great idea. They decided to meet at the Tavern for dinner. David and Lou thought that would be a good time to discuss this as a family. In one sense, it did concern everyone. However, they knew the girls would wonder why they went off to talk. At six o'clock, they all met at the Tavern. The baby was only a few weeks old. David missed him very much when he did not have time to stop over to see him. After they ordered, David brought up the dinner with Paulie they had planned for the following night. Julie would also be joining them. The girls thought that would be nice. David explained the conversation he had with Paulie. He wanted them to understand why he, Lou, and Paulie would be stepping out after dinner to talk.

Molly was never at a loss for words. She asked, "ARE YOU CRAZY?" Lou and David were not shocked by her response. They discussed how Ray did so much for them, and they had an obligation to help him if needed. David and Lou pointed out that Ray would have never found out all he did without them. It was a two-way street. At the time, it benefited everyone, and still could. If David took the case, he and Ray could not have any further discussions regarding any of the cases. When they broke it all down, it appeared that it should not be an issue. A situation always goes deeper than what appears on the surface. Lou suggested they discuss this with Ray. Not the details, but the concept and see what he thought. It would give them more insight as to how he felt regarding the matter. They decided that during the day tomorrow, David and Lou would call Ray and have a conference call to discuss it. They needed to know how this could affect their relationship in the future before they spoke with Paulie that night. They also had to consider that if their firm took Vincent's case, they could not be a part of representing Allie if the FBI called upon her to testify. Was that something they wanted to give up? Little did they know, these were minor issues as compared to what was about to come.

The rest of the evening was fine. Allie and David were lucky to have a baby who was always happy and did not cry a lot. The baby loved being around people in the shop. He was not bothered by all the attention. The hardest task was getting him to go to bed. He liked being around people. Lou and Molly could not get enough of him. At times, David and Allie felt Molly and Lou were more like parents rather than grandparents. That was fine with them. They wanted the baby to experience family love, and be raised with family values. The following morning everyone had breakfast and left for work. David and Lou had early-morning appointments and one court case. Once they wrapped up their work, they would call Ray. This would be a difficult conversation but needed to take place. It would require total honesty. They put a call into Ray about eleven o'clock in the morning. He was not in his office. They left a message with his secretary. She told them she would have Ray call them back later that day at 2:30. The remainder of the day it was business as usual. David had to stop by the police department to see a client and wanted to stop by the shop to see the baby on his way back to the office.

The baby looked forward to seeing David when he stopped in the shop to see him. Allie and Molly were curious if they had spoken to Ray. David told them they would be speaking at 2:30. He would let them know what had been discussed. Molly insisted on wanting to know. She did not want any surprises when everyone was over for dinner that night. David left and went back to the office. John, the police officer that Allie was friends with and helped them in the past, was in the shop when David stopped in. David appreciated when he took the time to stop by. He knew Allie and Molly appreciated this as well.

Ray was very punctual. At exactly 2:30, Ray called Lou's private line. David also had a private line. Their staff did not have those phone numbers. They were strictly for David and Lou to give out to those they wanted to have them. After a bit of socializing and catching up, Ray asked, "So what can I do for you?"

David did not need to go over the past information since they were all part of those events. He jumped right in. Ray was aware of the relationship that David had with Paulie within the organization and the events that took place. David explained what Paulie had discussed with him.

For a moment, Ray was quiet. He asked David, "How can I give you an opinion. You know you can represent whomever you want. We believe in the law, but we are also here to make money. Remember, I was in private practice once as well. If you choose to represent him, which is your right, anything I say now could compromise anything we may be investigating. I'm not saying he is even involved."

Ray added, "This would place us all in a difficult position. Any assistance I may need in the coming trials could only come from Allie and Russel. You also need to understand that you nor your firm could represent Allie. It would be considered a conflict of interest if you took Vincent as a client. On the other hand, if Lou tried to represent her, I would also have to object. A quirky judge could rule that since you are partners, family, and in the same office, neither of you can act as legal counsel for Allie. Allie has no risks other than the possibility to testify and confirm any information she gave us in the past. We both know and agree, I would try to avoid that. Honestly, I do not envy your position. I will say this. Whatever you decide, will not affect our friendship or future relations. I believe that is what you are really looking to ask." David and Lou laughed because of course that was their main concern.

David added, "I need to figure out a way not to do this. Ray, I am a criminal defense attorney. If Allie never attempted to clear her name and attempt to get her conviction overturned, I would have never been a part of it. I would take on the new client. However, that is not what happened. For me, and I think Lou would agree, it's not the right thing to do." Lou and Ray both agreed.

Ray stated one very important fact. "Speaking hypothetically; if the issue with Vincent is part of our investigation, you could help Paulie by having him become a federal witness. With the information Paulie might have, he could get into the program."

David replied, "Hypothetically. I think we all know that Paulie would never do that."

Lou and David looked at each other and now knew that Vincent was part of Ray's federal task force investigation. They both thanked Ray for his time and advise.

Before they hung up, Ray added, "David. At some point in the future, we will be sitting on opposite sides of the table. I am good with that. That is what we do. However, off the record, just between us, do you know what you're going to do in this case?"

David replied, "One way or another, I will be making a decision tonight. I will let you know what I have decided tomorrow. I am going to try every way possible not to do it." Ray respected that answer.

Lou told David the decision was his. He would support whatever choice he made. However, he agreed they needed to get out of this situation. Lou reminded him of a comment he made to Ray once during the initial investigation.

"David, do you remember what you said to Ray months back when all this was going on?"

David replied, "Yes. I told him I felt more like a prosecuting attorney than a defense attorney."

Lou smiled. They both agreed on what needed to be done. They called the girls and let them know about their conversation with Ray. It was a matter of courtesy, not a necessity. They were a tightly woven family with no secrets, and this concerned everyone. Allie and Molly knew this. They would support any decision David made. It was clear that they all agreed that David had to find a way not to become involved with Vincent.

Molly said, "Dave, as much as I love Paulie, this was the life he chose. He could have walked away when you did. He chose not to. You cannot feel responsible for that choice. Once these cases are over, you can help him in the future. For now, I think you are making the right choice. Can you live with that?"

David replied, "Yes mom. I can. You are right."

Since everyone would be there at 6:30, Molly told them she and Allie were leaving early to go home and start dinner. They would all meet at home. Six o'clock arrived, and Paulie arrived with Julie. They all chatted and played with the baby for a while. Allie put the baby to bed while Molly put the food on the table. Dinner was great as always. While the girls started to clean up, David, Lou, and Paulie went into the den and closed the door.

David started the conversation by asking Paulie to go over everything. He asked him to tell it all. Paulie explained he had no idea what the issue was. Vincent sent the message down that he wanted to retain David to represent him. Paulie told them he did not know why. That was the truth.

David said, "Paulie, I owe you. You know that. Without knowing what the issues are, how could I say yes, especially if Vincent had anything to do with all the crap that happened at the "Barn?"?" Paulie understood the problems that could arise.

"Dave, I'm not that high up on the food chain to talk directly with Vincent. You know that."

David asked, "If I don't do this, how does this affect you?"

Paulie replied, "It really shouldn't, but I have no idea why Vincent didn't have his people call the office directly instead of asking me to talk to you."

David explained he needed to obtain more information to make the proper decision. He asked Lou and Paulie if they thought it would be okay to call Max. Max was the go-between for Vincent.

Lou said, "I can't see where that could hurt. It may help to get Paulie out of the middle if you play your cards right."

David decided he was going to call Max. He had his contact information stored on his cell phone from the old days. He dialed Max. He answered his call. David told him Paulie was with him but had no idea what this was going on. He asked him to shed some light on it. He explained to Max that he could not just take on a client without knowing what the issues were.

Max informed David that Vincent heard some rumblings on the streets that some shit was going down with some people in New England. He might need a good lawyer to represent him and asked for you.

David said, "Max, it's no secret. It was all over the news I was part of that investigation. How can I take Vincent as a client? Two things would happen. First, no judge would allow it. It would is a conflict of interest because of the information I know from the older cases. Second, Allie, who is going to be my wife, was acquitted. Even if the judge allowed it, I could not represent her if needed. Max, this is a huge no can do. You know that."

Max replied, "David, what can I tell you, the man wants you."

David said, "That won't help the man if I get disbarred again, and that could be a real possibility."

Max explained, "Vincent knew this and would protect you, but he had to ask.

David said, "Max, let me ask you a question. How do you propose that I play both sides here? It's just impossible, and this is assuming what Vincent heard is true?"

Max replied, "Do you have any ideas?"

David asked him to tell Vincent, "If anything came up, and it had nothing to do with the New England cases, I would take him as a client. However, if it does, the legal system will not allow it. The prosecutor would object. If the judge denied it, the prosecutor could ask for a second ruling. Everyone's hands will be tied. I cannot, and will not, run the risk of getting in trouble again.

David said, "Max, talk to Vincent. Tell him what I said. I think that's a fair compromise and let me know."

Max replied, "Will do, I'll call you soon, and by the way, congratulation's dad."

David replied, "Thank you, I'll wait to hear from you."

They hung up. David's phone was on speaker. Paulie and Lou thought it went well. This should get Paulie out of the middle.

David said, "I didn't want to say no, and I wanted to put the ball in Vincent's court."

Lou said, "Well you certainly did that, now let's wait and see."

Lou told Paulie he wanted to speak with David privately for a moment. Paulie left the room.

Lou told David, "Well this all must be getting close to happening. With Ray knowing this, I doubt if he is going to tell us much."

David replied, "Damn it. I know. I don't like being in the dark on this shit."

Lou replied, "Let's take it one day at a time. Let's get back to our company."

The rest of the night went well. Paulie would be heading back the next day and probably would not see David until the christening a month before the wedding. When Paulie and Julie left, David explained everything to Molly and Allie. They did not say anything. Lou and David could tell they were concerned.

CHAPTER 3

WHEN IT RAINS, IT POURS

A week passed. David received a call from Max. Max told David he spoke with the boss. He explained that the boss felt this was a good compromise since the choices were limited. Everyone knew that a judge would never allow David to represent Vincent with all the information he had from the past cases. That would be ludicrous. The family felt more relaxed now. The next two weeks went by normally. The baby's christening was this Sunday, and Paulie would be back in town on Saturday. David did not hear from him since his last visit. That was normal for Paulie since his calls came in spirts. The wedding plans were complete. They were having a church wedding. The reception would be in the main ballroom at the hotel in town. A new luxury hotel was in the process of being built, but would not be ready until next year. Allie was very busy with her clothing line. She and David decided to take their honeymoon later. They planned to go into the city for a few days after the wedding. See a show, do some shopping, and return. There would be many guests at the christening and the wedding. They estimated over two hundred and fifty guests at each affair. A week before the christening, Russell called to let Dave and Lou know that Ray had called him. He wanted to set up a conference call up with them. Ray set a time and date that they all agreed to.

It was Monday, and the call was scheduled for Tuesday morning at 10 A.M. Lou and David would find out how much Ray wanted them to know. David never informed Ray about his conversation with Max. It was getting close to the christening and wedding. Lou and David did not want the girls to worry. They agreed not to tell them anything further. Allie was busy planning a fashion show to show off her fall designs. The dresses and accessories were starting to arrive. The show was scheduled for the week after they returned from New York. Allie sent out invitations to every major buyer and magazine editor. Almost everyone replied with a positive response. Allie and Molly were as nervous as they were excited, but they were doing it right. They planned a cocktail hour with appetizers before the early evening show. After the show, there was a party with a buffet dinner. Allie planned to book a floor at the hotel for those who wanted to stay the night. This was not about making more money. They were well off already. It was about a dream. If any of their children wanted to be part of the family's businesses, they would have a legacy. Allie and Molly wanted to make a huge splash. Allie and Molly shared the same dream. Molly always hoped it would be with Jessica, but by now, Molly became attached to Allie. Since Molly looked upon Allie as a daughter, this fulfilled her dream.

Tuesday morning Lou and David were sitting in the smaller conference room when Russell's call came in precisely at 10 A.M.

Ray started the conversation. "I think it's only fair for me to tell you where we are in this process. First, I have to ask David a question. Dave, where are you at with this Paulie think?"

David told Ray everything that happened, what they discussed and did, including the phone call with Max.

"Are you good with that?"

Ray replied, "I see no conflicts. However, it is a moot point. Vincent is involved. Thank you for being honest. I have a confession to make."

Lou replied, "We're all ears."

Ray said, "I already knew of your conversation with Max. Max is not his real name. He has been an FBI agent planted in that crime family for the past five and a half years. It took that long for him to gain their trust. Until now, with the cooperation of the "Judge," they could never put enough together that would be worth making an arrest. I now have all the pieces to the puzzle. Vincent will go down for sure this time. He will never be a free man again."

Ray went on to explain that much has happened. There were two attempts made on the "Judge's life." They both failed. The "Judge" was being held on a well-protected military base under complete lockdown, which made it nearly impossible for anyone to get to him. He went on to tell them to sit back. What you are about to hear will shock you.

Ray explained this was now joint FBI, ATF, and DEA task force. No one other than those involved knew who was on the team. It was a guarded secret for obvious reasons. Every agency received information from their sources and combined notes. Every video confiscated was reviewed and cataloged. The "Judge" had provided them with bank account numbers, shell companies, offshore accounts, as well as the location of the New England and New York ledgers. All of this information was correlated and combined. If all went as planned, they would have enough to send the head of the New York, New England, and Florida crime families away for life. About the blood we found in the "Barn," we also know who the victim was, and had proof of who committed the murder. All of this was tied to prostitution, drugs, weapons, and more. No one ever imagined this would turn into something much larger than anyone could have anticipated. They were still compiling additional evidence. If this all came together, this would be the single largest raid and arrest in the history of crime families, and all the agencies involved. The key was to have all the federal warrants issued. When the time came, they would be executed simultaneously. They did not want to give anyone a chance to warn others. To date, it cost the government millions to put this together. However, seizing of assets, money, and property, would easily return that amount and much more. All three agencies had a meeting with the federal judge at the end of the week to submit their briefs required to obtain all the warrants under special circumstances. They did not expect that would be a problem. They expected to plan the raid sometime in the following week. This would also have to be coordinated with all the local police departments with next to no notice. They had no idea of who could be on the crime family's payroll.

Russell, David, and Lou were in awe of all of this. No one ever came close to thinking this would be so big coming from a basic case of clearing Allie of her murder conviction. They all thanked Ray for the update and wished him good luck. Ray was coming to the baby's christening with his wife. They would talk more at that time. Ray hoped to get the warrants issued as soon as this Friday. The warrants were tricky because they needed to be worded in a manner that allowed them the freedom to search as needed. The day the warrants were going to be served, all bank accounts would be seized, except for those in countries where the United States did not have those agreements. However, the state department would be involved and put some pressure on those banks to get them to cooperate. These were months in the making, and thousands of hours and overtime was spent. It was getting close to the time this would all come together and pay off. They would place the bosses in military barracks in different locations for protection up to and during the trials. All others arrested would be held locally and in different locations. Once this happened, they knew there would be those seeking to make deals rather than being a target. They wanted to keep these people separated.

After the call, David said, "Son of a bitch. Now I know why that compromise went down the way it did. I would have never guessed when I spoke to Max he was an undercover FBI agent. He played the role well."

Lou just nodded his head and said, "Son. This is going to get real. Are you ready?"

"As ready as I'll ever be," David replied.

*****

It was the Sunday of the christening. Lou and David knew they could not discuss any of this with Paulie. David hoped that Paulie was not involved thinking he was new to the organization and low on the food chain. Most of the cases revolved around the "Barn," and started well before Paulie was involved to this degree. However, Ray was not just going after the "Barn," he was going after the organizations. It could get down to Paulie's level. Ray and Russell were at the christening with their wives. The girls would all be mingling, which would give the men time to chat. The church ceremony was beautiful. They had a traditional Catholic ceremony. The town people all made food for the gathering after the christening. The church hall was the ideal place to host the party. There was no talk about the case before the ceremony. Earlier that day, Paulie asked David if the issue with representing Vincent was resolved. He had not heard anything further about it. David told him it was taken care of.

Although this day was for family and the baby, David and Lou knew that they would be talking to Ray and Russell at some point later in the day. The party was from one p.m. to five p.m. There would be music, food, and dancing. Some came for a short while and left. Others stayed. It was a great opportunity for everyone to socialize. At the end of the day, everyone would pitch in to help clean up. About four p.m., Ray asked David, Lou, and Russell, if they could talk briefly. Lou suggested they step outside and talk for a moment now. There were many people there. No one would miss them. Paulie would be coming back to the house, and it would be difficult to talk there. Lou, David, Ray, and Russell went outside. Everyone lit a cigar to celebrate the day as Ray started. He explained he did not want to take a great deal of time. He felt everyone should be prepared.

"We will execute the warrants at the same time. It will involve multiple raids in many cities that will happen simultaneously. We will all be conversing through a dedicated satellite link. It will be the largest cooperative raid between the FBI, DEA, and ATF in history. If it worked, it would be epic."

Ray did not tell them the day, times or places. Russ, David, and Lou told him they would rather not know. Ray was very excited about this. Ray held his present position with the FBI for some time. He was ready to move up the ladder. Something this large would be his ticket. The opening he wanted would be coming available soon due to his boss retiring. Ray told them that many of the smaller fish would roll over to avoid going to prison. He was relying on that to fill in the gaps in the cases to make each one rock solid. They had to have every loophole covered. These crime families had the best attorneys in the country on retainer. They would look for anything to get them off the hook.

Being concerned, David asked, "Is it possible that Paulie does not have to be a part of this? We are best friends, and he is my son's godfather. In a short time, he will be my best man. Did you forget that Paulie was the one that obtained the pictures when I needed them?

Ray replied, "I know Dave. I remember. I cannot make any promises. The best thing for him is to become a witness for the prosecution."

"That answers that question," David said.

"Which question is that?"

Dave replied, "Will these arrests get to Paulie's level within the organization?"

Ray said, "Dave, I can't say. You know that. We have to use whatever advantage we have. If that happens, the choice would be his. If it gets to him, and he doesn't turn, I will speak to the judge and let him know how much he cooperated, which was part of what led to all these findings."

David thanked him but was still troubled by this. David assured him not a word would be mentioned. Ray replied, "If I were worried about that, we wouldn't be having this conversation."

They wrapped up their talk and started back inside. On the way in David said to Lou and Russell, "I have a bad feeling about this. Paulie is going to be arrested. I know it." They both agreed.

About 4:30, Ray informed Lou he was going to head back. Lou wanted him to come back to the house, but Ray thought that was not a good idea since Paulie would be there. They understood. He and his wife said their good-byes and informed them they would see them at the wedding. They reminded David and Allie to contact them when they were in town after the wedding so they could meet for dinner. David told Ray he could count on it.

*****

The wedding was now only four weeks away. Allie was very happy. She already fit into her gown. Lou and David still agreed not to tell Molly and Allie what was going on. People were starting to leave, and much of the cleanup had already begun. Lou had a small dumpster put in the back so everything could just be thrown right in. Russell, his wife, Paulie, and Julie were the only ones coming back to the house. The day was over, and everything was cleaned up by 5:30. They got back to the house about 6:15. Everyone sat in a chair to relax. It was a long day. Molly had already had the coffee pot set to have coffee made when they got home. Everyone made a cup of coffee and sat in the large family room. Russell and his wife were not going to stay long. They had to head back to the city and pick up their children on the way. They chatted until about eight o'clock and decided to call it a night. After their guests left, David, Lou, Allie, and Molly, stayed up talking until nine o'clock about the day. Everyone was tired. Allie and David went home. The baby had been sleeping in his car seat. The trick would be to put him in his crib without waking him. Any mother will tell you that never works out. The baby woke up, Allie fed him, and he fell back to sleep.

Allie and David were passionate and very much in love. It had been a while since they had made love since Allie was healing from the birth. They could not wait for Allie's doctor to give them the okay. They described their lovemaking as each time feeling like the first time. They believed if they made that effort their romance would never die. Although they were not officially married yet, they had been together for a while now and promised never to let that spark die.

While lying in bed, Allie asked David, "How long do you want to wait before we try for a little girl?"

David laughed and said, "Are you kidding, you haven't fully healed from this one yet."

"I know," Allie said. "I can handle it when the doctor gives us the okay. Were both almost thirty-seven and we're not getting any younger, and you know your mother can't wait."

David replied, "I know. When the doctor says we can, we will. I'm ready."

Laughing, Allie said, "Oh really? Are you horny baby?" She reached down to touch him, and she knew he was more than ready. "You know, there is more than one way to please each other or have you forgotten?"

No further words needed to be said. It was the first time they had been together like this since the baby was born. After they shared their intimate moment together, Allie explained they needed to get back to being themselves. As busy as they have been, they always must make time for themselves. She missed these moments. David agreed and replied, "You're right." Allie told him all he had to do was say something. She would have pleased him. David replied, "I know honey, but you know me. This isn't a one-way street." They agreed that having a baby changes your life schedule. However, when it came to their intimacy, they agreed they have to make time for each other. They both curled up and fell asleep. David was tired and not thinking about what was about to come.

*****

It was Monday. David had a full day in court. Lou had some meetings, and the girls were busy finalizing all the details for the fashion show. As opportunities go, this was a great opportunity for Allie. Over the weekend, she received the remainder of emails. Every buyer she invited was going to attend as well as representatives of the major fashion magazines. This week she and Molly were interviewing models for the show. Allie's designs were both contemporary as well as traditional with a country outdoor flair. Getting the right face for each ensemble was critical. The look of each model must match the look of what they were wearing. Thanks to the check she received from the government, she was paying above the standard rate because she wanted to see the best. On Wednesday, she and Molly were going into the city to conduct the interviews. They started at ten o'clock in the morning. They were putting the line together to take with them. It included dresses, sweaters, shoes, and other accessories. Charles, the firm's driver, would drive them into the city. At first, they were going to go the night before, but Allie did not want to leave David alone with the baby overnight. They usually took turns when he got up. When he was on more than bottles, he would start to sleep the entire night.

The grand ballroom of the hotel was exquisite. It was the perfect place to hold the fashion show. Many large companies rented that room for their conventions. The surroundings were breathtaking;

it was elegant, and the staff were friendly and accommodated their guests. If the show went well, and they received enough orders, Allie could start hiring additional staff. She had her eye on a building outside of town that came up for rent. It was large enough but needed cleaning and some modifications inside. It would be the perfect spot. It had a large room for laying out design tables, four offices, and a conference room. The building could be a great location for their corporate headquarters. Lou was handling the transaction for the girls. The timing was perfect. The building would be available two weeks after the show, and it would not take much to get it ready. The question that Allie and Molly now faced was whether to anticipate a good show and hire two additional staff members. If they did that, they would be there for the show. This would be a great training experience, and they would have a better idea as to the company's vision. These opportunities were excellent for older models who have reached an age where their modeling careers were almost over. Many wanted to stay in the industry. They were looking for these types of opportunities. They expected to get many applications since these opportunities were rare.

That night at dinner, the girls discussed this with Lou, since he was their lawyer, and his accountants handled the books. Lou set up the Allie M. brand, the copyrights, and patents. This was Lou's area of expertise as well as real estate. It was not a difficult task to accomplish. Although the corporation was not solvent enough yet to do this, the family certainly had enough money to support it. Allie and Molly needed to discuss this idea with the family.

Lou explained there are no guarantees in business. It is all about timing and product. With that said, if you get orders and cannot fill them, or have the staff to handle the business, it could lead to disaster. If this is really what both of you want, and you are going to do this, go big, or go home. David and I will certainly support you in every way.

That was it. The family made a joint decision. The girls would hire an account specialist and layout designer. They already had the computer software set up for ordering, and any required forms were printed. The buyers could easily place the orders at the show. The outsourcing manufacturing was all set and ready as well. Everything was in place. What they needed now, was a successful show. Since it was summer, that market was gone. Allie would be introducing the Allie M. fall and winter lines.

After dinner, while Lou and David were playing with the baby, the girls decided they would hire an agency to screen those interested in the positions. That would save them by not having to interview those who were not qualified. The best agency was in New York. Since they were going to be there in two days, they thought they would call tomorrow to see if they could meet with them when they were in the city. The people they hired would have to be willing to relocate to their area. Commuting from the city each day was not realistic. They would also have to be able to travel when necessary. These were good-paying jobs. They did not feel these terms would cause a problem in finding staff. These were exciting times. Meanwhile, David and Lou were filled with anticipation knowing at some time this week all these raids would take place. Between the wedding, the fashion show, as well as what would come out of these raids, David and Lou knew any involvement on their part if needed, wouldn't be until long after all these events had passed. They needed to focus on the next five to six weeks.

*****

It was Tuesday morning, and Allie and Molly were preparing to go into the city the next day. They had two appointments. One would be to interview models, and the other with the employment agency. They were eager to come onboard. Paulie and Ray knew they were going to be in the city. They both wanted to take them to lunch. The girls were not sure if they would have the time. They decided they would stop by and say hello to each of them. It would be much easier. They did not want to leave the city too late since they would have such an early-morning start. The company limo was very comfortable. They could nap on the way to and from New York. It would be about a four to five-hour round trip drive depending on traffic. As much as they were excited, they were not looking forward to the drive. Before David and Lou left for the office, David told them it was ridiculous to drive that much in one day, and have two meetings. All because Allie did not want David to have to get up with the baby every time he awoke. David explained, when she returned, it would be late. The same situation would exist the following night. He would have to get up so Allie could sleep. He and Lou insisted that they go into the city today, stay overnight, get some rest, and do what needed to be done the following day. These were important decisions, and they both needed to be fresh and alert. After going back and forth, everyone agreed. They would wrap up things at home, pack the limo, bring the baby to daycare, and head into the city.

Lou said, "Great, I'll call the hotel and make the reservation."

The girls wrapped things up and got into town around noon. They had a quick lunch with the boys and headed into the city. As it turned out, this was a much better plan. It would be the first-time Lou and David would have the baby without either of the girls. Lou stayed at David's so they could take turns getting up that night. As luck would have it, the baby only woke up twice in the middle of the night. They both got up each time.

On Wednesday, they called to let the girls know everything was fine and wished them luck. They brought the baby to daycare and went into the office. Around 4:30 p.m., the girls called to tell them everything went great, and they were on the way home. They did not get to see Ray because he was not in his office, and Paulie did not answer his phone. They would catch up when they got home if they were still up. Lou and David were happy they had a good day. They got home about 6:15. The baby was fed at daycare. They spend some time with him and put him to bed. They had dinner delivered at the office and ate there. Around eight o'clock, Lou's phone rang. It was Ray. The raids went down. Between New York, Florida, and an undisclosed area in New England, seventy-six people were arrested and taken into custody. More arrests would be coming. He told them they found everything they needed and more. It was a total success. Everyone was taken completely by surprise. They had all been under close surveillance for some time now. They knew where everyone would be and when. It went like exactly as planned. Ray was extremely excited.

David asked, "I have to know. Was Paulie arrested?"

Ray replied, "I would never lie to you. We arrested Paulie."

David said, "Jesus Ray, he's supposed to be my best man, and he did so much to help us before."

Ray said, "Calm down. I get it. We all know he will not turn. That is not his character. Like you, I feel I owe him something. If I don't arrest him along with the others at his level, it will look like he informed. I am only charging him with racketeering and prostitution, no drug charges. As much as I know his crew deals, I do not have enough to make that stick. I did you a favor. You know he will call you. You can represent him on these charges without being tied to the bigger picture. He only has one prior along with probation. You should be able to get him off with a stiff fine and probation, which I will support. Honestly, most of these smaller fish will be out on bail in a few days. It will take time for all of this to go to court. I am trying to have revoked for the bigger bosses. We know they will skip. You will have plenty of time. Any involvement on your part, if needed, will not be until long after your wedding and Allie's show has passed. Relax."

David took a deep breath and replied, "Thanks. I owe you big time."

Ray said, "Yeah I know." They laughed and hung up.

David was quite relieved as he felt his heart pumping in his chest. He would now have to wait for a call from Paulie. It was the evening. With all the processing that was required, Paulie probably would not call until tomorrow. He could not call him or the station. He knew Paulie was smart enough to keep his mouth shut. He has been in this position before.

Lou laughed and said, "Your face went as white as a ghost when Ray told you he arrested Paulie."

David replied, "I'm just glad Ray is helping me with him." Lou explained that he thought that he would. Ray could not forget that Paulie helped in the other case. Ray owed him one and did the right thing.

David said, "I know dad, but it's different when it is closer to home."

Lou asked, "Why are you still looking concerned?"

David said, "I don't know. I have a feeling that something is not going to go right. I can't put my finger on it."

"Well then," Lou said, "We are just going to have to stay in touch with Ray, keep Russell in the loop, and watch as things develop."

David felt that anyone who turned here is going to be a target. Lou agreed and explained, anyone who turns will be placed in protected custody. Paulie will not turn. You know that. David explained that was not what he meant. David told him he was concerned if Allie has to do any testifying, he did not want her caught up in all of this.

Lou said, "Don't blow this out of proportion Dave. If Allie has to testify, it will only have to do with "The Crew" that framed her for murder. She will not be a part of the rest of this. I think due to all the evidence Russell presented in the first case which cleared her, and all that Russell found during the process, Ray may not even need her, but I understand your concern." Lou went on to say, "At the time; we time, we looked at this from every possible angle. Calm down. You have a wedding coming up. This should be a happy time, not a time for worry."

David said, "Well, at least we know why the girls couldn't reach Ray or Paulie today."

They were both tired but wanted to wait for the girls to get home. They knew they would be excited and want to tell them everything that happened. They turned on the TV, and both fell asleep in the recliners. About two hours later, Allie and Molly arrived home. Hearing the limo doors close woke them up. They walked out to greet them and help with their bags. Lou tipped Charlie because it was a long two days for him. He gave him tomorrow off so he could get some rest. Lou was happy to have Charlie. He was great and always there when Lou needed him. Lou took good care of him.

Charlie thanked him and said, "I hope you guys took a nap because they slept most of the way home."

Lou laughed and said, "We figured they would. Good night and thanks again."

The girls were excited and could not wait to tell them how everything went. The short story is, everything went great. They picked out six models for the show and met with the agency people to start the job search. They had lunch and stopped by to see Ray, who was not in his office. They thought he was in court. Allie explained they tried calling Paulie a few times. Each time his phone went straight to voicemail. They left a message, but he never called back. This was not the time to tell them what had taken place that afternoon. They knew the time had come that they needed to know, but this was not the time. David was concerned Allie might hear about this from Julie. He felt they should hear it from him and Lou first.

Molly and Allie were so beautiful and feminine; at times, Lou and David forgot how tough they could be. After all the updates, David and Lou thought it best to tell them. He knew they could handle anything. Tomorrow Julie and the girls would be in the shop, and Julie might know by then. David and Lou told them everything that took place that day, including the conversations at the christening. They were a little upset that they did not tell them sooner, but they understood the reasoning. The boys were surprised when the girls said they were expecting this. It was getting late. Everyone said goodnight and started to bed. Allie stopped in to check on the baby and decided to unpack and get it done. The clothing from the fashion line was dropped off at the shop on the way home. They would take care of that in the morning.

It was about 1:30 am when David's cell phone rang. It woke up Allie, but not the baby. The baby usually got up wanting to be fed or be changed around two a.m. It was Paulie.

"Dave, I'm sorry to wake you this late. I was arrested. There was a huge takedown today. I can't tell you how many guys got pinched, but they got Vincent as well."

David said, "Paulie, let's talk about you. I don't want to know about anyone else."

Anything Paulie told him would fall under attorney/client privilege, but David wanted to maintain plausible deniability. Which means, if he does not know anything, he cannot testify to it, especially since he was part of the original case. He asked Paulie what the charges were.

Paulie said, "Nothing drug-related, just racketeering and prostitution." David knew that Ray had told him the truth when they spoke earlier.

Paulie asked, "Can you represent me on these charges?"

"I could represent you on these charges. I will not represent anyone else. Please do not offer my services to anyone. Do not say a word without me being present. When are you due in court?

"Not until Friday, will you be here."

David replied, "Of course. I should be able to get you out before the weekend. Can you make bail?"

Paulie replied, "That's no problem."

"Sit tight. I will call the station and tell them I am representing you. They won't bother you after that, and we will talk later today."

Paulie thanked him. He apologized for calling so late. David called the station to inform them Paulie had an attorney. Contact him first if they intended to question him. He would be there late tomorrow.

Allie heard the conversation and asked, "What are your plans?"

"I'll drive into the city tomorrow afternoon. I will stay overnight and go to court on Friday. I will try to get him released for the weekend. I'll be back later that day."

Allie said, "Why don't you have him come here?"

David replied, "I doubt that the court would let him go out of state, but he would try since Paulie's family and attorney are here." They went back to bed.

Even though everyone had an earlier nap, the day before was stressful, full, and long. Everyone awoke exhausted. After getting the morning routine out of the way, Lou and David headed to the office. David told Lou about Paulie's call on the way. David explained he would be going to the city. He planned to leave around noon so he could meet with Paulie. I will stay overnight, go to court in the morning, and come back after court. David told Lou he wanted to get Paulie out for the weekend and ask the judge if he could stay with his family.

Lou said, "Good luck with that. I'll call Charlie to drive you in."

David said, "No. You gave him the day off. He had a long two days. I can drive myself. That is why I took my car. You can go home later with the girls."

"Are you sure? Charlie won't mind."

"Yes. I am sure. If all goes well, I should be back early in the evening. I plan to ask Ray to have Paulie's case heard first. I was going to call him anyway. You know dad; Ray kept his word."

Lou replied, "Why, did you think he wouldn't?"

When they got to the office, David called Ray and told him he would be representing Paulie. Ray told him I knew you would. David thanked him and told him he was going to be in town by six p.m. so he could meet with Paulie. He was staying overnight and would go to court in the morning. He asked Ray if there was any way Paulie could be seen first so he could get an earlier start back.

"I can arrange that. We could bypass the court part if you want and put this together."

David said, "I would love that, but for appearance's sake, let's do it by the numbers."

Ray agreed. David said, "I need to ask you one more thing."

Ray said, "What's that?"

"How do you feel about Paulie being able to stay with his family? It would be certainly easier for me since we would be in the same town."

Ray, replied, "Let me think about that. If we don't want it to look funny, do you think that makes sense?"

David agreed. They decided to think about it and discuss it further later. Ray told David he was also staying over the night because of the long day he would have in court tomorrow. He suggested getting together at his hotel for dinner after David met with Paulie. David thought that was a good idea as long as Ray did not mind a late dinner.

Ray said, "Any time I get to have dinner, I feel lucky. I do not care what time it is." They laughed, and David told him he would text him when he was in town.

David stopped by the shop before he left to say goodbye to Allie, Molly, and the baby before leaving for New York. While driving, he received a call on his cell phone from an unknown caller. It was a man representing Vincent. He asked if they could retain their law firm to represent Vincent. He explained the FBI arrested Vincent. David explained that he had spoken to Max about this a few weeks ago. He explained they both understood that due to his involvement in earlier cases where the evidence could overlap, the judge would not allow this since he was aware of certain information that could be connected to this case.

The man, who did not leave his name, said, "Vincent won't be happy about this."

David said, "There is nothing I could do about it. The law is quite clear on this matter. The prosecution would object to it anyway. The judge would have to rule against it."

The man went on to say, "What if I told you we could fix that problem?" David replied, "Look. I was disbarred once because I helped Vincent. It took months for me to get my license to practice reinstated. If I lose it again, I will never get it back. I heard some rumbling's as to what happened. No one is going to take any chances. I don't know the details, but it seems big."

The man asked, "Then why are you heading to New York to represent Paulie, and you won't represent others?"

David asked, "How do you know that?"

The man replied, "We know everything."

David said, "Then you should know that Paulie's charges are minor, and have nothing to do with the other case he was involved with months ago. Paulie's charges are local and not federal. Vincent's charges are probably federal. Without knowing the charges and everything involved, I told Max that if the cases were not related, I could represent him. If they are, I cannot. He spoke to Vincent, and he understood that."

The man said, "And?"

David said, "You know I'm going to the city for Paulie; I will look into Vincent's charges. Understand that I can't do anything if the charges are related to a previous case where I was privy to any information."

The man said, "You have my number on your caller ID. Call me and let me know."

David asked, "By the way, why isn't Max calling me, he told me he was the go-to guy for Vincent?"

The man replied, "I can't say, you will probably hear about it and hung up."

There was nothing to check on. David already knew everything after talking to Ray. The suggestion that Max was an FBI plant for years is why he did not hear from Max. He hoped to avoid this type of situation. The last thing he wanted was problems. He would not risk losing his license again, or betray Ray. There was a larger question to be answered. If the same judge that helped them in the past were handling these warrants, why would he rule to let David represent Vincent? David was very troubled by this. Was there more corruption? It did not make sense. David had to decide whether to tell Ray about this when they met later. He decided to call Lou and explain the situation.

Lou said, "I'll call Ray to give him a heads-up on this. You can talk about it tonight. If you want, make it a conference call from Ray's secure line, and the three of us can discuss it. In the meantime, don't get involved with anything."

David said, "I have no intentions of doing that."

Lou told him he would call Russell as well. Maybe it was time for him to look into a few things. He might be able to find out who made the call.

"Good idea. I recorded the call. I will call you when I meet up with Ray."

Lou said, "Good job recording it. We'll talk later when Ray calls."

Both David and Lou were troubled about this. They were not concerned about anything happening to the family. They thought that was not an issue. They were wondering why this was coming up again? They were not comfortable not knowing who this man was. David thought Max was Vincent's right-hand man. Since Max was an agent, he might not be in the loop anymore after the arrests took place. Who was this man? They were curious about his statement regarding the judge. How many people were in Vincent's pocket? David was thinking, When it rains, it pours.

CHAPTER 4

GAME TIME

David ran into traffic and arrived at the police station shortly after six p.m. He called home to let Allie know he was there. When they spoke, Lou asked to speak with David. Lou told David that he and Ray spoke. Lou explained to Ray about the phone call. Ray informed him they would discuss it when they met. They decided to make it a conference call. David asked Lou to tell Allie he would call her when he got back to his hotel room later that night. He sent a text to Ray and informed him he was in town and at the police station. He added he would call him when he finished his meeting with Paulie, and they could meet for dinner. David did not check into his hotel yet. As he was walking inside, he ran into two attorney's he worked with at the firm where he was previously employed. They chatted for a moment. They were telling David he was a legend in the office.

Laughing, they said, "You pulled a doubleheader. Not only did you get your privileges back, but you also managed to get Allie's case overturned. Everyone was impressed."

As it turned out, they were representing some of Vincent's people. The senior attorney was handling Vincent's case personally. They told David not to be surprised if the lead attorney called him. In their meeting about the cases, they discussed trying to have David join Vincent's legal team.

David replied, "Really," and played stupid.

This town was full of cutthroat, backstabbing people. You learned not to trust anyone. Since his old boss did nothing to help defend him or stand beside him when he had his troubles, David would never work with that firm in any capacity. They parted company, and David went inside. Many of the officers were on the job for years. David knew most of them. He asked if he could meet with his client. David reviewed the charges. They were local, nothing federal. Ray did him a big favor. They showed David to a room and brought Paulie in. Paulie was happy to see him and thanked him for coming. After the police questioned Paulie, he and David spoke.

Paulie said, "David. What the fuck is going on? How big is this? The word on the street is, the bosses in Florida, New York, and New England got pinched."

David replied, "I can't discuss that if I'm going to represent you, and if you are smart, you'd stay as far away from that as you can. Get my meaning?"

Paulie nodded to express that he understood. He got the message.

"Paulie, there were no federal charges filed. These are local charges. They are charging you with racketeering and prostitution. You are lucky. The last time you were charged with racketeering, we managed to have the charges reduced to illegal gambling. I am hoping due to that, I can get you off with probation and a fine. It will probably be stiff and come with community service. What do you think?"

Paulie said, "Are you kidding me? I would take in a heartbeat."

"There is no way to get any of these charges reduced because they have your ledger of accounts. Therefore, it's no longer illegal gambling."

"Paulie replied; I know. I'm good with that. Can you get me the fuck out of here tomorrow?"

"The bail will probably be high. Can you handle it?"

Paulie said. "No problem,"

David told him he could possibly have him out by noon. He added, "Because I came in from out of state, I requested you to go before the judge first so I can get back. Who do you want me to call to get things ready for your bail?"

Paulie gave him the name and number of the person to call.

"I'll take care of it as soon as I leave. Don't be surprised if the FBI asks you to testify."

Paulie replied, "No way. I am not a rat. Besides, I wasn't that high up in the organization to know anything about that crap."

"How do you feel about us trying to get the judge to allow you to stay with your family with an ankle bracelet? Would you come home? It would be easier since we would be closer."

Paulie replied, "I would love to get away, but I'm afraid that wouldn't look right to the others."

"Ray and I thought of that as well, but I had to ask. The time to ask would be when we are in court."

Paulie said, "Thanks for thinking of me, but I think it's best if I stay local, plus there are other considerations I have." David did not ask what those were.

David went on to say, "Before I leave, let's go over what will happen tomorrow. The charges against you will be read. You will be asked how you plead. Plead guilty. The judge will set your bail and assign a sentencing date. I will have the person posting your bail ready. Although the charges are local, the local prosecutor will be working closely with Ray. I am sure many other people are getting charged with local crimes as well as federal crimes. I am confident I will be able to get the deal I want. You did help in the other case. Ray did not forget. Are you sure you are okay with this deal? If they had not found your ledger, we could fight it. With that ledger, we have no grounds for a defense."

Paulie replied, "I know. I was stupid for leaving it around. I should have known better. Let's do this." David reminded him not to speak with anyone without him being present and left.

When he got into the car, he called Ray. David told him he on his way to his hotel. He asked Ray where he was staying. As it turned out, they were staying at the same hotel. David told him that makes it easy. I will check in and call you from my room. We can go to dinner. It's my treat. David got his room number and told him he would call him later. When David got into the hotel, he checked in and went into his room. He called Allie to check on her and the baby. He spoke to Lou and told him he was meeting Ray for dinner, and they would set up the conference call when they were seated.

Lou replied, "I spoke with Russell. I'll fill you in later."

David took a few minutes to freshen up and called Ray. He left to meet him at the restaurant. They met and asked for a table in a private corner. It was around 8:30. Ray was busy most of the time preparing for tomorrows day in court. He did not realize how hungry he had gotten until they sat down. They did not order cocktails. Neither of them ate. They went right to ordering appetizers and food. They briefly spoke about Paulie. Ray informed him that everything was all set for the morning. Paulie was not that big of a fish in the pond Ray was trying to empty. Everything would go as planned. David remembered he forgot to call the bail bondsmen for Paulie. He took a minute and made that call. The bail bondsman informed him he would be ready. He would already be in court for some of the other men who were arrested.

When that call was over, Ray called Lou on a secured line and added David to the call. Everyone agreed how Paulie's case was being handled. David would have to go back to court for the sentencing hearing.

David said, "Since everything is ready to go, I might send one of the other attorneys to handle the formalities since we are in agreement."

Ray said, "That's fine, but let's talk about your phone call."

David took a deep breath and said, "When the call started, I hit the record feature on my phone to record the call." He explained the entire call to Ray.

Lou added, "I called Russell and asked him to try to track the call and find out who this was."

Ray said, "You all got my drift about Max right?"

David said, "Yes. Nice work by the way."

Ray said, "He is going to be a key witness for me in Vincent's case because he was close to him. I still cannot believe how Allie's case was the thing that started this ball rolling. It resulted in all these additional arrests. Everything that Russell uncovered tied it all together. My people could take over now. I hear there was a bounty on Max and not the good kind."

David asked, "What the hell is Max going to do afterward this case is over?"

Ray said, "His story is pretty sad. He buried himself in work after his wife and unborn child died. During her pregnancy, Max's wife developed a bleeding disorder. They considered her a high-risk pregnancy. Max, (which was not his real name), was at work one day. She was up on a stool dusting a ceiling fan in the kitchen when she lost her balance and fell. She broke her hip when she fell and bled out internally. By the time she dialed 911, and they arrived, she was gone. He was never the same after that. He volunteered for this undercover assignment. He was undercover for just over five and a half years when this investigation took off months ago. In the last six or seven months, he started to get very close to Vincent and became his right-hand man. He had to do some very bad things to get to that level of trust."

David and Lou were shocked when they heard this. Ray said. "He will either go into the program, which he claims he will refuse, or we will send him overseas, or somewhere far away. He will get a new identity. No one will know who he is. We will give him a new employment history and get him out of here so he can stay with the bureau. At least, that's what he said he wanted to do."

David said, "He sounds like the type that if he doesn't work, he would probably kill himself over grief."

Ray replied, "You're probably right. The job is what kept him going. Can I have one of my tech people take your phone while court is in session and download the recording? Maybe they can do a voice match."

"Sure, I want to be able to head back right after Paulie goes in front of the judge. I want to beat the Friday traffic."

Ray said, "No problem. I will have the IT agent at the courthouse. He could do it right there. It will take less than five minutes."

The food came, and they continue while they were eating. Ray did not get into the intimate details. He told David and Lou, the less they knew, the better. Every case they had on each of the bosses was rock solid. Many heads would roll.

Ray laughed and added, "We confiscated more money than we gave Allie just from some small-time hoods."

David laughed and replied, "Well, you could always give her more."

Lou agreed. The less they knew, the better. Lou asked, "What do you think the chances are that Allie may have to testify?"

Ray said, "Let's be clear on this. I know you are both concerned about this. The only testifying anyone would have to do would be to confirm any statements already in evidence from the original case, which caused the FBI to get involved. Their defense attorneys may not even want to cross-examine anyone since these facts are already verified and in evidence. If the attorneys could agree that a confirmation testimony is not needed, then they will never have to be involved. That is my goal. This will be going on for some time. Plea bargaining will certainly occur, and people will turn over rather than go to prison. The key is going to be to get the court to let them hold the bosses without bail. I believe they are flight risks."

They ended the call, and Ray and David finished dinner and agreed to meet at the courthouse around nine.

David went back to his room and called Allie. It was about 10:30. She was already in bed, but not asleep. They were like two teenagers telling each other how much they missed each other. David briefly explained the night and told her to get some sleep. He would call her when he was on his way back tomorrow. If all went well, he thought he could be home by six o'clock. When they hung up, he called Lou to see what he thought of the conference call. Lou was awake expecting David's call. They agreed this should not be a big deal. Lou told David that Russell was looking into who called him.

David said, "Dad. I wish I could shake this feeling. I know something is going to come up. No offense, but you have not seen a lot of this type of shit. I have. People don't take this lying down."

Lou replied, "I know, stop worrying. Wait and see what Russell and Ray dig up on this guy. Get some sleep, and I'll see you tomorrow."

David had a feeling that turning Vincent down was not going to turn out well. Vincent was not the type to give up and did not like taking no for an answer. David knew he trusted him since he never blew the whistle on them when he was disbarred. Vincent played David and Paulie to get that evidence removed so he would get off. He used them because they owed money for gambling and drugs. David thought to himself, how could he have been so stupid? No matter what, he could not be caught up in this again. He rolled over and finally fell asleep.

He was up early and got his things together. He had the room until eleven and left his things in his car. When he returned, he could leave. He left his car in the hotel lot and took a cab to the courthouse. He met Ray at nine as they agreed. The IT tech agent was waiting when he arrived. In minutes, he had the call downloaded into their system and headed back to the office to isolate the two voices. They would run a voice recognition match on the man who called. If they were lucky, they might find a match in the FBI database. They also had access to the NCIC, Interpol, and other databases. They had many recordings from all the wiretaps and surveillance they had done over the past months. It was worth a try. Ray told David they would let him know if they came up with a match.

They reviewed Paulie's case quickly. The court convened at ten sharp. Paulie was the first case. When Paulie's case came up, they all stood up. Paulie pleaded guilty to the charges as agreed. David requested reasonable bail since Paulie did not have a significant criminal record, the charges were not federal, and he was not considered a flight risk.

The judge asked, "Does the prosecution have any objections or concerns before I set bail?"

The prosecutor stated, "No objections your honor."

The judge stated, "Regardless of his record, these are serious charges, and there is significant evidence. I am setting bail at $50,000."

David thought that was high, but was not going to rock the boat and risk pissing off Ray or the judge. Paulie said he could make bail. The sentencing date was set for just under three weeks. David would try to finalize a sentencing agreement before that time which would be recommended and presented to the judge. Although the judge has the final say, they usually went along with any agreed the prosecutor and the defense attorney made. Paulie's bail bondsman was in court and handled the formalities. Paulie was free to go. Everything went as planned. David stayed until Paulie was released. Paulie's driver was waiting for him outside of the courthouse. They gave David a ride back to his hotel, and Paulie thanked him.

David said, "Forget it, we are family. Do not be late for the wedding, and stay the hell out of trouble. Anything you get in trouble for could jeopardize getting you out of this mess clean."

Paulie said. "Not to worry. Soon, you will understand why."

The valet attendant brought David his car, and he left. He called Allie to tell her he was on the way home. It was close to one o'clock, and the traffic was getting heavy. On the way out of the city, David suspected someone was following him. He kept looking in his mirrors and saw the same car three or four cars back. It made every turn that he was making. He made a couple of wrong turns to see if the car still followed. It did. He did not want to panic and call Ray. He thought once out he was out of town, they would break off. If not, then he would make a call. As he entered the parkway, he got a flat tire and had to pull over. When he pulled over, the other car also pulled over, but the occupant stayed in the car. The man in the car sat there watching. David got out and started to change the flat. While putting the tire in the trunk, he noticed a piece of glass was stuck in the tire. He wanted to remove it. He didn't want to leave it in and forget it and cut himself when he removed the tire. When David was retrieving his fishing knife from his toolbox, the man got out of the other car. David was watching him through the rear window and noticed he was walking toward the back of David's car.

When he came to the back of the car he asked, "Do you need some help?"

David said, "Thanks for stopping, but I'm all set." The man was well dressed. David just stood there with the knife in his hand.

The man said, "That's a nice fishing knife. I had one similar to it when I was younger." His voice sounded familiar to David.

The man asked, "Did you think I was following you?"

David replied, "To be honest, yes."

"I was. Ray wanted to be sure you got out of the city alright."

David played stupid. "Ray who?"

"You know, Ray, the FBI guy."

David knew this was bullshit because no agent would call another FBI agent "The FBI guy."

David asked, "Why would he do that?"

"Beats me, I do what I am told." He started to walk away.

Suddenly, it came to David. He recognized the voice. That was who called him about representing Vincent. He wrote down the license number and called Russell when he got back in his car. He left, and the other car had already left. He wanted to call Russell first and thought he would inform Ray later. Ray was going to be in court all day and probably would not be available. He did not call Lou. He did not want the family to worry. He told Russell the story and gave him the license number. He swore him to secrecy. Russell told him he would not say a word and would get back to him shortly.

The rest of the trip home was fine. No one was following him any longer. David knew this was a message. A way of letting him know he should help Vincent, and they knew where he was and what he was doing. About an hour from home, Russell called and said the car came back registered to a shell company. It only existed on paper. He was going to put someone on it and get photos of anyone who drove the car. He told him not to worry. If they wanted to send a more serious message, they would have done it then. Most times this was a way of getting someone to think, and be scared. In this case, maybe get David to consider helping Vincent.

David said, "I'm not scared for me, and I'm not representing Vincent. Should I tell dad?"

Russell said, "Yes. I will take care of Ray. I hope between the pictures and a voice match, we can ID this person. Dave, you are getting married in three weeks, focus on that. I'll take care of this."

David finished the drive home and was tired. Naturally, he ran over every possible scenario in his mind the rest of the way home. David was thinking about his family. He knew Russell was right, but he still had a feeling he could not shake. When he arrived home, everyone was happy to see him. He said everything went well. He spent a little time with the baby since it was close to his bedtime. They got him tucked in, and they had a bite to eat. While the girls cleaned up, David and Lou went outside for a cigar. He told Lou what happened. Lou was mad that David did not call him right away. Lou was Italian. As soft-spoken as he was, he could have a temper when provoked. He did not like this at all. David explained what Russell said. They both knew that Ray needed to know but would let Russell handle it. The rest of the weekend went fine until Sunday night.

*****

David got a call from an unknown number. He was not going to answer it. He never receives calls labeled as unknown. The firm had their cell phones set up in such a way that their numbers were completely private. Only four people in the firm had company cell phones - Lou, David, Molly, and Allie. They only gave out their numbers to people they knew. Lou was strict about that policy. When David was not answering, the caller kept calling. When he decided to answer, he was glad he did. It was Paulie. He was calling from a burner phone. Paulie did not want the call to be traced back to him.

David asked, "What's up. Why the burner phone, I am your attorney? It wouldn't look funny that we spoke."

"The rumors are flying within the organization. I know we can't talk about it, and I'm not asking to; I'm just letting you what I heard. As for the phone, I don't trust anyone. Maybe my calls are recorded."

David said, "Okay, that makes sense. Paulie, when all this is over, you have to start rethinking your life choices. One day, I am not going to be able to get you out of a mess, especially now that your record is starting to get worse. Luckily, you have no felonies yet. The truth is, this last one should have been. We both know Ray cut you some slack. Don't you think you should consider switching sides?"

Paulie said, "Why, only to have to move somewhere with a new name and identity and never be able to speak to those I love again? Sorry, that's not for me. I have been thinking about getting out for a while. Now is the best time to try since many are jumping ship. I don't know what I would do for work."

David explained that since the firm had become busy with criminal cases, he and his dad had been talking about putting on a private investigator. Even though they used Ray, they felt it was time have an investigator on staff for the smaller cases. With no felony arrests, Paulie could consider doing that, or possibly get a job with Russell.

Paulie said, "We can talk about that when this is wrapped up, but that's not why I called. Dave, did someone follow you the other day?"

David said, "Yes."

"Tell me what happened." David explained the story to him. Paulie said, "I guess what I heard is true."

"Paulie, don't tell me any details, just tell me what you heard."

Paulie said, "Your life is not in danger so relax. I just heard that Vincent wants you to defend him. He knows he can get it approved. He is trying to scare you."

David interrupted and said. "There's no way he can. Ray would never allow it. Vincent might be able to buy a judge, but never Ray."

Paulie replied, "I know, but if the judge says you can, Ray can't stop it. The glass in your tire was put there in the parking garage. The man who approached you was a way of sending you a message. Vincent was not going to stop trying. I can't tell you who the man was because I don't know. Until you just confirmed it, I was not sure if the rumor was true. All types of rumors are flying. Everyone is running for the hills. Is this that big?"

David replied, "Paulie, all I can say is; it's much bigger than you can imagine. Get out of this as soon as you can. When this is said and done, the future is not going to be good. You can end up in a situation you can't get out of."

"I know," I know. I have to work on that."

David said, "We'll support you, don't worry. For now, sit tight, and stay out of trouble for the next 2 and a half weeks. Get past the sentencing and put it behind you. If you get caught up in anything higher and get arrested, I may not be able to represent you."

Paulie said, "Okay, thanks. We'll talk soon."

Shortly after he hung up with Paulie, he was updating Lou when Russell called. He told them he had some photos and sent them to Ray. I hope with the photos and a voice match, they can identify this man.

Lou said, "Okay, keep us in the loop," and hung up.

Everything was in chaos now. David and Lou knew this would be the best time for Paulie to get out. The organization had little to no money coming in. They could not do business. It could be like this for some time. David told Lou this was going to get ugly. Russell told them he sent five pictures to Ray of people who they witnessed drive that car. They hoped Ray would have more information in the next day or two.

On Monday, Ray called to say they did not find a voice match but identified all the men in the pictures that Russell had sent him. They were going to bring each of them in for questioning and record their voices. This was a way for them to get a voice match. They hoped that one of them would be the man who approached and called David. Later that day Ray called to inform them they were all picked up for questioning. Tomorrow they would know if there was a match.

Ray said, "I don't think there is any reason for anyone to be concerned. David, what do you think about trying to get in to see Vincent? I already put some things in place. I have your name on a list of people that are not allowed to visit or speak with him due to a possible conflict of interest. There will probably be more than one judge handling these cases. I do not want them to have any grounds to request an appeal. They still can, but they would need a good reason. In the meantime, I can get a judge to place an injunction denying you to talk with Vincent due to the previous cases and your involvement. It is the law, and there is a clear conflict of interest. You could call this man, and tell him when you are going to see Vincent. I am sure he has his way of getting messages to Vincent. When he finds out, you cannot get in. We hope he will tell Vincent. Maybe that will get him off that path. No other judge will overturn that injunction. It would raise too many questions."

They thought that was a great idea. Ray added, "If we get a match, I will let you know, and we'll set the trap. Meanwhile, tomorrow I will get the injunction in place."

That was the plan. Now it was time to sit back and wait. The minor criminals were held locally, and the three big bosses were at different locations under complete lockdown on military bases. Anyone who wanted to visit them had to be pre-approved before they were allowed in. They had to schedule their visits in advance. The authorities monitored and recorded all calls except the ones they had with their attorneys. The only private calls allowed were to and from their immediate family members. David, Lou, Russell, and Ray, were smart men. The key would be staying one step ahead of the game. David placed a call to the man who called him. He told him he would meet with Vincent. They choose a day and time. The man told David he would get the message to Vincent through one of his attorneys, who would also be there as well. They set a time to meet the following Monday at ten a.m. David had to drive to upstate New York to see Vincent. It was a much shorter drive. David let everyone know the arrangements. David knew this was a wasted trip. He knew he was not going to get in. This was strictly for appearances.

*****

The rest of the week was uneventful. Everything was in place for the wedding. There was nothing left to do but wait. Allie and Molly had a couple of people coming in for interviews that week. They spent their time wrapping up the plans for the fashion show. They wanted to have everything in place before the wedding. David and Allie were only going to the city for four or five days. The fashion show would take place a week after they returned. Molly could certainly handle any last-minute details. The models were coming into town the following week for their final fittings. Catering, music and the party afterward was already set up. They had a gala event planned. There was a great deal happening all at once. Everyone was starting to feel overwhelmed. David and Lou still did not tell the girls about all the recent events. They did not want them to worry. They felt there was no need to let them know all of this at this point.

It was Thursday, and Ray sent a text to Lou setting up a conference call at three p.m. that day with everyone. They expected to hear news about the man who followed and called David. They were correct. The call came through right on time. Lou, David, Russell, and Ray were on the call. The photos Russ sent to Ray did the trick. The man's name was Joseph Rivera, who also went by other aliases. His rap sheet was a mile long. He had been arrested for breach of the peace, assaulting an officer, gambling, and attempted murder, which was dismissed due to lack of evidence. He was an enforcer for the family. Between the pictures sent by Russell and the voice recordings when they were brought in for questioning, the plan worked. David had already identified him by the photos Russell had. The voice match confirmed it. Ray only brought the others in as a decoy. They found an outstanding warrant on him for some minor violations and arrested him while he was there. They let him go with a "promise to appear" in order not to cause suspicion.

David said, "I'll update you all on Monday regarding my visit with Vincent."

Ray told him he was sorry he had to make a wasted trip knowing you won't get in. They all agreed this was something they needed to try. Vincent's attorneys would be meeting him there. They hoped this would work.

Ray said, "Let's have an understanding. There can't be any further secrets. If anything happens, anything suspicious, or something that concerns you, call me right away."

Lou made it clear that the girls still knew nothing of this. They wanted it to stay that way. Everyone agreed.

Ray said, "I'll talk to you Monday. Let me know how it went, or should I say, didn't." David replied, "No problem."

The baby was getting big, and was now on soft foods and sleeping better. They planned to go out to dinner that weekend and unwind from all these activities. The wedding was only two weeks away. Business was good, and the weather had been great. This was the towns busiest summer tourist season in a few years, and it was only halfway through the season. All the businesses in town were very pleased. Saturday night everyone went to dinner. All Allie and Molly talked about was the wedding. Allie could not wait for all this to be done. They had a nice honeymoon planned during the fall or winter. They wanted to go somewhere warm. Vermont was very cold during the winter. By then, they would need a vacation. They had a great weekend. There was an event in town they would all be going to after church. David had to leave early Monday morning. Lou insisted that their driver take David. He did not want him to be alone. Lou had some very large clients. Many times his driver would pick them up and return them to the airport when they came to town. He would drive their wives around while the men played golf or fished. His driver was not busy every day, but always found things to do.

Lately, he was running many errands for Allie and Molly. He welcomed the opportunity to take David. Charlie was a retired Navy Seal and served for thirty years. He had a good pension and did not need to make that much, but Lou paid him well. He was married once but got divorced while he was in the service. His wife could not take him being away so much and met someone else. She was very honest with him. They divorced and stayed friends. He did not want to hold her back. He was not going to leave the Seals. They did not have children, which made it much easier. He lived just outside of town. This was a perfect job for him. When he retired, he did not want anything stressful for work. He felt he went through enough stress in the military. He was living with his girlfriend for the past five years that he had been working for Lou. By this time, they were like part of the family. His girl was a local girl he had met after he was discharged. He came to the area for a vacation. They met in town, and the rest was history. They hit it off. She was also divorced and had no children. They were at an age that they would not have any children and were happy living together.

It was Monday morning. David and Charlie left bright and early. No matter who Charlie drove, or where, he never asked questions. They would talk of course, but he never pried into the matters of business. He was very spiritual and was quite active in town. He was an assistant coached for the baseball team as well. He was quite the player himself. He once had an opportunity to get on a major-league farm team but turned down the offer to join the military. His whole family served. It was a tradition. He was a third-generation seal. Not having any children, that tradition would now end. Being a seal is a tough life. Not just for the team, but also for the wives and family. There were support groups, but it was still very hard. The law firm sponsored many things in town for their young adults. Charlie and David had a lot to talk about on the drive. When they arrived at the base, Charlie did not have to ask any questions. With his background and clearance, he knew what the purpose of this base was. Since the base was on lockdown, checking all visitors, as well as their vehicles, was a requirement each time anyone wanted to get on the base. Two jeeps escorted every vehicle. One in front and one behind the car, each jeep had two MP's. They escorted them where they had to go, and when they left. One of Vincent's attorneys was waiting for David outside the building they had to go into to see Vincent. They chatted for a bit, and he filled David in. They always got along when David worked in the city. David's issue was not with the other attorneys. It was with the senior partners. The attorneys just followed orders.

Any visitor had to go through another security checkpoint before they got to the main desk. Once at the main desk, they would have to show their ID's again and sign the logbook. When they were done, the MP at the desk checked the list. He explained to David that his name was not on the approved visitor's list.

Playing along, David said, "Didn't your boss get this cleared?"

He replied, "I thought he did, let me call him."

He called the senior partner. He called the prosecutor's office while he had his attorney on hold. They informed him that David, nor anyone representing his firm, could visit Vincent due to their involvement with previous cases. According to the law, this would be a direct conflict of interest in these new cases. The prosecutor's office told him he would send him the court reflecting this.

The senior partner got back on the phone and said, "It's not going to happen. There's a court order preventing David, or anyone from his firm, from having contact or represent Vincent."

David played the game and said, "I came all the way up here for this? Make sure you tell Vincent I tried. I told his man that this would never happen."

David left. With a little luck, this would make Vincent stop trying to get David to represent him. He got into the car, and he and Charlie started back. He called home to let them know he was on the way back. He informed Lou what had taken place and asked him to tell Ray.

David and Charlie stopped for lunch on the way back, then finished the drive. David stopped at the shop to see Allie and the baby, then went to the office. Paulie's case was up for sentencing next week. He planned to send one of the junior attorneys but thought it was best he go himself. He knew Paulie would feel more comfortable if he were there. Paulie called him later that day from the burner phone to tell him things were starting to fall apart. Everyone was out for themselves. No one knew whom to trust. Many people were brought in for questioning. Out of those arrested, many were being arraigned tomorrow. Paulie knew more than David did. Ray was not telling Lou or David any intimate details. All the seconds in command were running things. Without any books or records, it was a shit show. The only people who knew who owed were minor players like Paulie, and only if they still had their books. Small change compared to the income that came in from all the larger sources. Everyone was having trouble paying up. Everyone was afraid to do business since everyone was under surveillance. The other families wanted no part of this. David told Paulie to stay clean. His sentencing was next week, and the wedding was the week after. This would probably get worse.

"Are you going to the sentencing or sending someone else."

David replied, "I will be there. I will be talking to Ray to figure out what the sentence will be. I could be two years' probation, two hundred hours of community service, and possibly up to a fifty thousand dollar fine. I'll try to get the fine reduced, but the reality is, if they confiscated everything you have, which they could, you would be in worse shape."

Paulie said, "Do the best you can. I can handle it. I have to figure out how to get the hell out of this lifestyle. It feels good when everyone makes you feel important, caters to you, and you have a pocket full of cash, and you can get any woman you want. I am getting older and have other things going on. This is getting old. I can recognize the warning signs. If I stay with this, it probably will not end well. I never see my family." Jokingly he added, "Maybe if I get out your father will hire me as an investigator."

David said, "Don't joke about it. That could be much closer to happening if you get away from these people then you think. See you next week." They hung up. David was in court most of the remainder of the week. Lou was busy setting up contracts for one of their largest accounts.

*****

Meanwhile, Allie and Molly were busy. They interviewed six people for the two positions they wanted to fill. There were coming back four for a second interview. With the wedding less than two weeks away, they wanted to get this wrapped up. The girls wanted them to start when David and Allie returned from the city. That would give them a week with them before the fashion show to get them semi acclimated to their goals and vision for the company. Allie and Molly worked together like a finely tuned machine. One or the other could handle things and make decisions for the business and the clothing line. It helped that they had a Julie as their store manager to run the day-to-day business. As big as the shop had gotten with the expansion, they always kept the personal touch. The regulars like John, Allie's police officer friend, Jeff, the Chief of Police, still stopped in for coffee and a chat. No matter what, the girls believed they needed to keep the core values that made their business successful. Every business in this part of town was like that. Like all towns, as the outskirts of the town grew, so did some of the issues, but the town kept those on a short leash. The town had a reputation for being family orientated, safe, and clean. That is what drew people there. Under no circumstances would they compromise that. Things such as adult bookstores or anything with porn was not allowed. Every employer had a liberal dress code that employees followed.

The town still believed in family values and professional ethics. If people wanted that type of entertainment, wanted to see servers in hot tight tee shirts, this was not the place to go. Many wealthy people had A-frames or hunting cabins. Some owned property along the lake and were only there for the summer.

It was time for David to go to the city for Paulie's case. He had already spoken with Ray and knew what the plea sentence would be. They did have to negotiate some of the finer points, but he should be in and out. Paulie would receive two years' probation, two hundred hours of community service, and a twenty-five-thousand-dollar fine. Before court started, Ray and David met with the judge to go over the sentencing terms.

In his case with his record, the judge stated, "According to the sentencing guidelines, I could sentence Paulie to a minimum term of two years in prison and up to a maximum of five years. Since there is an agreement in place, and instead of jail time, I am going to add one additional stipulation. During his probation period, he is not to have any contact or involvement with individuals with any arrests or convictions of the same charges, or any individuals convicted of any felonies. He cannot associate with those involved in with any known criminal organizations. Any violation of these terms would revert to the maximum prison time of five; less time served on probation."

David took a minute to discuss this with Paulie. Ray or David did not foresee this. Paulie did not have much choice. He would either agreed or go to jail. David informed the judge that Paulie agreed. David asked the judge if Paulie wanted to move out of the city for a job opportunity, which would also assist him in not being in contact with this element, would that be acceptable.

The judge said, "I will leave that decision in the hands of his parole officer who could make those arrangements."

They went into court, and all went as planned. It was over. In the hallway, David told Paulie what he had told Ray earlier. "Paulie, the judge did you a favor. He gave you the opportunity to get out of this lifestyle. Don't be stupid, take advantage of it. You have one week to think about this before you have to report to your parole officer."

"There is nothing to think about Dave, let's make this happen."

David said, "I'll make the arrangements before you meet with your parole officer if he allows it." They left the courthouse.

New York is a huge city. People always get lost in the system. The only way to get Paulie out of this was to get him away from it. As a favor to Ray, the parole officer agreed to meet with Paulie and David the following day. David would stay overnight. It was good David would be staying. It gave Paulie and David a chance to have a serious talk. Paulie had some things to do some things. David thought it would be good to stop and see one of their larger clients in the city. PR is the name of the game in corporate business. He made plans to meet Paulie for dinner around six at his hotel. He called Lou since they had some things to discuss. It was only 11:30 in the morning. David got a hotel room and called Lou. Lou was not shocked by the details. David asked to know why. Lou asked him not to be mad, but Ray knew the judge was going to add this piece. They had that arranged. With everything going on, he forgot to tell you. Honestly Dave, so did I. This is the best thing for Paulie. David was not mad. He knew Lou was right. He told Lou he was going to stop by the insurance company that was their largest client in the city. Introduce himself, and take them to lunch if they had time.

Lou said, "That's a great idea. I am working on something big for them now. This is perfect timing."

"Dad, a couple of weeks ago, we were talking about bringing on an investigator for the firm. We even mentioned Paulie. What do you think?"

Lou replied," I was going to discuss that with you tonight when you got back, but since you're staying over, let's take a minute now."

"What are you thinking?"

Lou said, "If you agree, I thought we would hire him and give him to Russell for a few months for training and building contacts. Possibly Russel may have a position for him and could assign him to us. Either way, we could get him home, keep him out of trouble, and help him get his life on track. One way or another, he would have a job."

"Wow. Great minds think alike. Thanks. I don't see this as a problem. I have had previous dealings with the person who is Paulie's parole officer. He is a nice person and really tries to help people get themselves straightened out. I am sure he would be willing to help. His caseload is probably quite large. Our parole officer back home has a much smaller caseload. Transferring this to our jurisdiction would be easy. Paulie was fortunate that the judge left it up to his parole officer. No court approval will be required."

Lou said, "I'll run it by Russell and call Clark." Clark was their local parole officer. "I'll see if he's okay with it, and get back to you with Clark's answer."

"Great. Maybe the two officers can talk tomorrow and get the paperwork started. I am sure that will take a couple of weeks. This will give Paulie time. I will run it by Paulie tonight. Dad, he's ready for a change."

Lou said, "Okay, we'll talk later. Let me know how your lunch goes."

David left his car in the hotel lot and took a cab over to their client's office. They were happy he stopped in and had time for lunch. It was a great meeting. It was the first time they met David since Lou informed them of the father-son merger. After lunch, David walked around and did some shopping. He wanted to bring something nice home for Allie and Molly. Lou called and told him everything was all set with Clark. He would be expecting a call tomorrow. David informed him the meeting went well.

Lou said, "Yes, they called me and thought it was a nice surprise. They were happy to meet you and very impressed. Thanks."

David replied, "No problem. They were very nice, and I should get to know our clients. We will talk later. Say hi to everyone for me." David bought a couple of things and headed back to the hotel to take a nap and wait for Paulie's call for dinner.

CHAPTER 5

WHEN YOU LEAST EXPECT IT

Later that afternoon, David received his call from Paulie. They made plans to meet at David's hotel restaurant at 6:30 for dinner. He was hoping Paulie would be receptive to the proposition of working with the firm. The meeting with Paulie's parole officer was at nine the next morning. David wanted to get an early start back and hoped the appointment did not take long. When David was shopping, he bought Allie a cute outfit at a lingerie store. He thought what he had picked out was sexy as hell. Allie's body was perfect. She looked beautiful in these outfits. He loved it when she came out of the bathroom wearing one. She did not do this often, but she knew when he needed that little bit extra. He was daydreaming about making love to her and having their next baby. He sent her a very provocative text. She promptly responded with one of her own. It drove him insane. She added she had seen the doctor, and she said they could start having normal relations again. David let her know he could not wait to be. He added he would call when he was almost home. He asked her to leave the shop early and meet him at the house. Mom and dad could bring the baby home. Allie loved that idea. Molly loved little cute things such as figurines, or something that had a special meaning. He found a small doll set. It was a grandmother and grandfather holding a baby. It sat on a nice piece of stained wood with the inscription, "Grandparents." It was a high-quality piece and a collector's item. He knew she would love it. For now, he only wanted to go home with Allie and make love to her. The wedding was only a week and a half away.

Whenever David traveled, he always brought a spare set of clothes. It was almost time to meet Paulie. He showered, changed, and left for the restaurant. Paulie was waiting at the bar. They sat for a few minutes and enjoyed a cocktail before they were seated at their table. For a hotel restaurant, it was known for having some of the best food in the city. David was in the mood for lobster. That was his choice.

David asked Paulie what he thought about the court that morning. Paulie had mixed feelings. He only knew one lifestyle for some time now. One he enjoyed but knew he had to change. Being raised together, Paulie and David wanted the same things. They had both been sidetracked for a while.

"You are a lucky man," Paulie said. "Part of me is jealous. I have never told anyone, but I have been seeing someone for some time now. She has no idea what I do for a living. I am too embarrassed to tell her. What I do is bad. It is illegal, and no good comes from it. She is nothing like that. She works hard and has been wondering where our relationship is going. Dave, this is something I have to do, not just for me, but also for her, and us. I am bringing her to the wedding."

David was very happy for him. David told him once this was all squared away, and should you decide to accept what I am about to offer you, you have to be honest with her to order to move forward. If you both love each other, there should not be any secrets. If she loves you, she will understand and respect your decision to make things right."

"I hope so. She has been wondering why I have never brought her to meet my family. I have met hers. They live in upstate New York, and she does not like city life. She had to take a job here because that's where the work was." David asked him what she did.

"She is a hotel manager for one of the largest hotels in the city. There aren't many hotels where she comes from, and they don't pay well. She is a country girl at heart."

David said, "Let's talk because I may have another idea."

"Let's do this. You have me curious."

David explained he and Lou spoke. If Paulie was interested, David knew the parole officer. David asked, "Do you remember Clark, the parole officer back home? I believe I can convince your parole officer to transfer your case file to Clark. He is probably so overwhelmed, he would be happy to let it go. The judge left it up to him to decide. Dad and I also talked about you coming on as an investigator. Paulie, we are all family. We have to help one another when we can. Dad already had the same idea. He thought if you were interested, he would talk to Russell and have you work with him for a few months to learn the ropes. If Russell has an opening, maybe he would hire you and assign you to us as a client. If not, we would hire you and have Russ train you." Paulie just sat and listened. David said, "Say something."

Paulie replied, "I don't know what to say. What would I do about my girl? I don't want to lose her."

David said, "How about telling me her name for starters."

Paulie laughed and replied, "Her name is Maria. She's 100% Italian."

"That's a beautiful name, and you get along?"

Paulie said, "Yes, she doesn't take any crap from me."

"I can't make any promises, but you know a there is a new luxury hotel is being built outside of town. The hotel should open in less than a year. They are starting to hire. I know they are looking for a manager. With her work experience, I know my dad can get her an interview. Besides, my dad sold them the property and was very instrumental in working with them and the town on some long-term tax breaks. He has connections with them."

Paulie's eyes were watery. "Dave. I am in love with Maria. I know how much she loves me. This has been eating at me for over a year. It would be awesome if this all worked out?"

"Anything is possible if you both want it. Look at what Allie and I have been through."

Paulie replied, "I'm going to have a long talk with Maria and tell her everything. If that goes well, I will tell her about what we talked about as well. I want to ask her to marry me. I already bought the ring. If you see her at the wedding, you will know it all worked out.

David said, "I have a feeling it will. Are you going to show me a picture of her?"

Paulie showed him a picture of Maria. She was beautiful. She had long dark-brown hair and was the same height as Allie. Paulie was an inch shorter than David was. Paulie showed him another picture of them together. They made a very handsome couple. She was two years younger than Paulie.

David said, "Everyone will be happy to meet her, especially your mother. If you come back engaged, your mother is going to be in shock."

Paulie said, "Mom has been bugging me for some time now to find a girl and settle down."

"She is not wrong you know. Will you text me her picture? If I don't show it to Allie before the wedding, I'll be sleeping on the couch."

Paulie sent it to him. The rest of the time they laughed and talked about their high school days and all the things they got away with. It was 9:30 when they were ready to leave. David suggested Paulie spend the night with him at the hotel. Paulie thought it was a good idea. They were both tired and had to get up early. David had two beds in his room. When they arrived at David's room, Paulie called Maria, and David called Allie. Allie was with Lou and Molly. They put him on speakerphone. He told them about Maria and sent the pictures to Allie. Everyone was very happy for Paulie. David was teasing Allie and Molly telling them he had a surprise for them. The girls hated when he did that because they always wanted to know what it was. When they were all done chatting, Dave and Lou spoke privately. David told him how things went with Paulie.

Lou said, "Don't worry. Tomorrow I will call the hotel group and see where they are in the hiring process. I will tell them about

Maria. They probably will not hire a manager until they have the opportunity to meet her."

David thought she probably has a resume. Lou gave David the email address where Maria should send her resume. If everything went well, Maria would be attending the wedding. Since Maria would be in town, that would be an ideal time for her to schedule an interview with the hotel representative. Lou explained that he spoke with Russell. Russell does not have any openings now, but if Lou wanted to hire Paulie, he would train him. If an opening occurred, Paulie could stay on with Lou, or transfer to his agency. Lou explained they would cross that bridge when they came to it. For now, the firm would hire Paulie and let Russ train him. David explained this to Paulie. He was excited and hoped Maria would be as well. It was late, and they had to be at the parole officer's office at 9 a.m. They turned off the lights and went to sleep.

David and Paulie were up at seven and getting ready for their meeting. Having breakfast was the first item on their agenda. The firm had an account at the hotel where they always stayed. They never had to go through a lengthy checkout. They took a cab to the office where the meeting was to take place. They arrived about 8:45. David did not know that Lou had spoken to Ray and asked him to reach out to the parole officer. Ray spoke to the parole officer earlier that morning. He informed him the government had no objections to the arrangement that would be presented, and he would email their approval to him. It pays to have connections. They were the first appointment, and everyone was on time. They met at nine sharp. It was straightforward. David explained the concept to the parole officer, including living arrangements and work. David explained that they needed his help in this matter to get Paulie on the right path and lead a more productive life. The parole officer was an understanding man. He always helped those that genuinely wanted to help themselves.

He said, "I have never received a call from a prosecutor supporting someone like this. I already spoke to Clark before you came in. He knew Paulie well and was fine with the arrangement. With this type of support, I see no reason to deny this since your firm is willing to hire him. Clark and Ray spoke very highly of Paulie.

You are doing me a favor. My caseload is overwhelming. Since the court has given me the power to make these decisions, I will grant the request. I will turn the file over to Clark by the end of the day. Paulie, allow me to make this clear. Once this file is turned over to Clark, you will become his responsibility. You will have to get your things in order quickly. You have to be there permanently, and meet with Clark in two weeks."

Paulie said, "That's not a problem. I rent a furnished apartment. All I need to do is pack my clothes and some personal belongings. I'll be staying with my mom and dad until I get settled into my own place."

The officer looked at Paulie and said, "Don't let me down son. Don't let Clark find out he made a mistake. Can you get it right this time?"

"Yes sir" Paulie replied.

Both Paulie and David thanked him. They shook hands and left. The whole meeting lasted about a half an hour. They were both quite pleased. David was curious as to how he was going to tell the others in the organization. Paulie explained that many of them were in court yesterday. They heard the judge's ruling and sentence. They are so worried about themselves; they don't give a crap about me. Most of them are already trying to get out themselves. We may be what we are or were, but no one wants to spend years in prison.

David asked, "Will you need any help?"

"No. If all goes well with Maria, he would be home by the middle of next week, and the wedding was the following Saturday. Maria took the week before and the week after the wedding off. I figured when you were in the city we might meet for dinner. Now, I won't be here."

David replied, "Don't worry. With all this shit going on, we might go up to the falls instead of the city. It is better if I am not around here right now. We are only going to be gone for four or five days. She has the show the following weekend, so she needs to be back on Thursday. We are planning to take our honeymoon over the winter so we can go somewhere warm."

"That is a good plan. You have been living together for some time now." When the cab dropped David off, he told Paulie to be sure to call him after he spoke with Maria to let him know how it went.

"We are meeting tonight to talk. The crazy woman thought I was breaking up with her. I laughed and told her I would never do that. I told her I thought it was time to talk about our future. She seemed excited about that, but then, she doesn't know the story yet."

David said, "Don't worry. It will be fine. Tell her the whole truth, everything. Call me and let me know how it goes. I don't care how late it is."

"I will. You're right. She needs to know everything to make the right decision for herself."

They said good-bye, and they would talk later. It was just past eleven. David had the valet get his car. He called to let everyone know he was on the way back. He told Lou that everything went well, and he would give him the details about Paulie when he got home. Lou had already known about the parole decision because Clark called him to let him know.

As it turned out, David would not get home as early as expected. He was stuck in traffic for a few hours. The highway was closed due to an accident. He let Allie know so she would not rush or worry. It would not make a difference. They will have their time together later that night. David arrived home around seven. He called when he was about an hour away. When he got in, dinner was ready. He took a minute to fill Lou in on how the lunch went with their client. When they all sat down to eat, David broke the news about how everything went with Paulie's parole hearing. Molly and Allie were happy and excited for him, and especially for his parents. His mom, dad, and Julie missed him very much. He told them about Maria. He had already sent a text with the pictures to Allie, who of course showed Molly. They could not wait to hear how his conversation went, and they all hoped it went well. Paulie was finally making some positive decisions about his life. Everyone talked for a while. The baby did not want to go to sleep, so he stayed up a little longer before he eventually fell asleep in David's' arms around eight-thirty. They put him in his crib and had coffee.

Lou explained that he had spoken to the hotel group. The HR representative was excited about Maria. They had not seen any potential candidates they would consider hiring for that position. She was looking forward to receiving her resume. She told Lou she would contact her to set up a time and date to meet when Maria was in town. At ten o'clock, Paulie called. He was very excited. His conversation with Maria went well. He explained she was impressed that he was honest with her and glad he was getting out.

David asked, "Did you ask her?"

Paulie replied, "Yes. She said yes."

David told everyone the news, and they all congratulated him. Paulie added, she was very excited about the prospects of this new hotel and emailed them her resume. Paulie explained that Maria wanted to return to the country life, and this would be perfect for them if it worked out. Either way, she was leaving her job and returning with Paulie.

Paulie said, "We'll figure it out when we're home. Dave, I told mom and dad. They were so happy and said they could not wait to meet her. I sent them her picture. They talked to her on the phone. They told us we could stay with them as long as we needed to."

"That's great. What are the plans regarding moving? When are you coming home?

"Paulie replied, "We are moving back this weekend. Maria received a free room at the hotel that came with her job. She has no furniture to move. All we have to bring back are clothes, minor household things, and personal items. Except for our clothes, everything else we plan to put storage. I am going to call the storage place outside of town tomorrow and rent a space. I am getting a small trailer tomorrow. I rented it for one-way. We can start loading it up. We should be in sometime late Sunday afternoon."

"Outstanding," David replied. "Let us know when you're about an hour out. We will meet you at the storage facility and help you unload the trailer, and help you get your things in your mom's house. It will go much quicker, and Maria will have some time to unwind. I'm sure on Monday you will want to take her around."

Paulie thought that was a great idea. They hung up, and David and Allie were ready for bed. David was thinking; this is going to smooth. Something has to go wrong. David gave Allie and Molly their gifts. Lou and Molly loved the grandparent's doll and teased Allie about her night apparel.

Lou said, "Babe, let's go home so Allie can get changed." They all laughed, and they left.

As tired as Allie and David were, they were not going to let this night pass them by without having some quality time. They took a nice hot shower together. Allie was quite the tease. David tried to start things many times in the shower.

Allie just kept teasing him saying, "No babe, let me change. You get into bed, and I'll be out in a few minutes."

David dried off and got into bed. Allie did herself up quickly and put on David's favorite perfume. The outfit he bought her looked fantastic on her. Allie thought it fit perfectly. David knew his wife to be. David was in bed and could smell her perfume. His hormones were raging. The anticipation was getting to him. He could not wait for Allie to step through the bathroom door. It seemed like a lifetime. Suddenly, the door slowly opened and out walked Allie. David thought to himself; she was perfect. No picture he had seen in any magazine came close to the way Allie looked. He had never seen a woman of such beauty. She slowly walked towards the bed. Turning as she walked. David could see every side of her body. She got on the bed and had him roll over. She gave him a nice back massage. The anticipation was killing him as she rubbed her hands firmly but gently down his back. He turned and started to take off her outfit.

Allie said, "No-no babe. I'll do it." She stood up on the side of the bed he was on, and slowly started undressing. As she was undressing, he caressed her body as each part became exposed. She turned slowly as each piece of clothing dropped to the floor. They both were thinking how sensual this was. Allie was finding it hard to continue. She wanted this moment to be special for them both to enjoy. It had been quite a few weeks since the last time they could make love in a way that he could penetrate her.

This moment could not have been any better. Allie and David were both excited. They could see it and feel it in each other. Allie did not get into bed yet. As she slipped her panties down to her ankles, David started to caress her thighs. When she kicked them off, she stood there. Her legs slightly opened as if she was inviting David to touch her. While he was touching her, she was also touching him. They were leading up to the moment when she would join him in bed. When she got into bed, their bodies just intertwined with one another as they kissed and touched each other so tenderly. As they kissed one another's body, they each had an orgasm. It was hard for them to hold back. They did not try. They had their times when they enjoyed a quickie or oral sex, but most times, they liked to take their time, and completely explore one another. The passion they were both were feeling would make this night one of complete exploration. After they relaxed, they were cuddling. Allie suddenly got on top of David and put him inside of her. She moved so slow and methodical. Allie certainly knew how to move. They were as one in bed. Like a finely tuned instrument, they liked the same things and knew how to make a moment last. David rolled Allie on to her back. He lifted her legs over his shoulders and penetrated her again. Kissing her and caressing her breasts. He also knew how to move, and knew what Allie liked. They could both sense when their time was near, and they wanted to have an orgasm together. Most times they did, other times one or the other could not hold it back. Either way, it was always wonderful, loving, and caring. Tonight, they were one. They could sense everything about each other.

As Allie and David neared their orgasm, they talked to each other to heighten the experience. David started to move faster and push harder, going deeper with each thrust. Seconds later, they exploded together. Moaning, groaning, and talking to each other as they experienced this moment together. This woke up the baby. They rolled over exhausted. The baby must have found his binky. He stopped crying and fell back to sleep. After they rested for a moment, they would cuddle and talk about how good they felt. To them, it was part of the romance and lovemaking experience. While they were talking, they were hoping the next time Allie got pregnant it would be a girl. If it were, they might try for another boy, or stop at two. They decided if it were another boy, they would try for a girl. They both wanted to give Molly a granddaughter. It was around 11:15 when they finally fell asleep.

*****

Meanwhile, Lou's and Molly could only imagine what Allie and David were doing. This caused them to become excited as well. They were also passionate people. They had been married for some time and never lost their passion and romance. They were both exhausted, yet in the mood. Tonight would be more of a quickie. At ten o'clock, Lou's phone rang. It was Ray. Lou had just started to fall asleep. Ray apologized for calling him so late.

Lou said, "No problem, what's up?"

Ray said, "No one has heard from Max for two days. He decided to temporarily transfer to another state until all this was over and he testified. He is staying with the bureau under a different name. He never boarded his flight, and he is not answering his phone. No one has seen or heard from him. We are concerned."

Lou replied, "Maybe he just needs some time. Five and a half years is a long time to be undercover."

"Let's hope so. If anything happened to Max, I swear …"

Lou interrupted and said, "Ray, you don't get it done with revenge. Put that on hold. Wait and see what turns up. If it's not good, get your revenge in court."

Ray replied, "You're right. Do you think Russell will help us with this? We are spread thin, and he has great resources. Many of which are better than ours."

"Of course he will help. Do you want to call him or would you like me to?"

Ray said, "We worked well together in the past, and I'd rather you and David not be a part of this. If you don't mind, I'll call him."

"I understand. Please keep us in the loop."

Ray replied, "I will. Thanks."

Molly heard this conversation and said, "Don't you dare bother David with this now. Let tonight be for them. You can let him know in the morning."

Lou replied, "I wasn't going to. Get some sleep. It's amazing the things that happen when you least expect it."

CHAPTER 6

ALL GOOD THINGS COME TO AN END

The next morning, Lou informed David of his call from Ray regarding Max. David said, "Shit, I told you I had a feeling something was going to happen."

Lou replied, "Let's not jump the gun and make wild assumptions. Maybe Max needs some time. After all, he lost his family and has been undercover for over five years."

Dave replied, "Maybe. I just have a bad feeling. I have had it all along. We'll see."

The next two days were routine for everyone. The wedding was only eight days away, and Paulie would be coming home this weekend. David did not want anything to ruin this time for Allie.

With everything that was going on, and David wrapping up a trial, David and Lou stopped thinking about Max. They did not hear anything more from Ray or Russell. On Sunday afternoon, David got the call from Paulie. He was only an hour away. The plan was David, Lou, and Peter, Paulie's father, would meet Paulie and Maria at the storage bin and help them unload the trailer. They would follow them to his moms and unload the reminder there. It would all go in the spare room, and Maria and Paulie would sort it out the next day and return the trailer. Allie, Molly and Paulie's mom Shelly, were at the house cooking dinner for everyone. They all would be meeting Maria for the first time. Shelly wanted Maria to feel special and welcome. Molly and Shelly were good friends. Paulie's was finally home to stay, which made his parents very happy. They never approved of what he did. They chose to ignore it rather than face it. Shelly and Peter owned prime land and built a beautiful home not far from Lou and Molly. Shelly and Peter owned and operated the custom craft shop two doors down from Molly and Allie's shop. Julie, Paulie's sister, never was interested in crafts. She attended an academy for beauty, skin, and hairstyling. When she graduated, she started working for Molly when the day spa was opened. Eventually, as the business grew, she became the manager.

Paulie and Maria arrived right on time. When they were all introduced, Maria felt very comfortable. Paulie had told her so much about everyone, she felt like she already knew everyone. David thought that she was much prettier than her picture. She was beautiful, not like Allie, but in her own way. They had two different types of looks. David could tell she was a country girl. They chatted for a short time and then started to unload the trailer. The storage bin was small. They did not have much that needed to be stored. They only had glasses, general kitchen items, dishes, and silverware. Since they had two apartments, there were many doubles. Paulie and Maria talked about living together a few times. The hotel room Maria lived in came with her job. She did not have to pay for it. At the time, she did not know what Paulie really did for a living. She thought he was in real estate. Due to his type of work, Paulie felt it was best if he kept his own place. It took no time to get the trailer unloaded. Lou called Molly to tell them they were on the way and would be there in twenty minutes. Dinner would be ready in an hour. This would give them time to get the trailer emptied before dinner, and everyone would have some time with Maria. Maria was a worker. She did not just stand there and watch. She got right in and worked as well. She was a full-blooded Italian girl. She knew how to work, cook, and clean. That was her upbringing. Like Allie, she was a strong and independent woman. You could talk to her. As warm and friendly as she was, anyone could sense she was the type that would take any crap. As the men were finishing the trailer, Maria met the girls and immediately started to help. The girls were talking. When dinner was ready, everyone sat down to eat. Everyone hit it off immediately. They felt like they knew each other for years.

Before everyone went his or her separate ways, David asked Paulie if he was okay financially, especially after having to pay that fine. Pauline told him he was fine for a while. Lou, Paulie, and David planned to meet on Wednesday to finalize getting him started. David would be back from his short time away before Paulie's first parole meeting with Clark. It was now up to Paulie and Clark to work out the details. His employment with the firm would be already in place by that time. Maria was impressed; she already received an email back from the hotel chain. They had a meeting scheduled for the following Wednesday and seemed anxious to meet her. If all went well, Paulie and Maria would not have to stay at his mom's that long. Everything seemed to be right on track. The wedding was less than a week away. Time would pass quickly. It was Wednesday before they knew it. Paulie left for his meeting at the firm, and Maria was ready for her interview. When the boys met, they made their offer to Paulie. They explained he would go with Russ for six months. Russ would get him up to speed on all the basics such as background checks, basic investigating, and interviewing techniques. Paulie would start at an entry-level salary, which would seem small compared to what he was making. The difference was; this was an honest and respectable living. He was fine with that. He would work with Russ at one of their satellite offices about an hour away, three days a week. The other two days he would be in the office with David and Lou. Lou already cleared this with Clark.

It was about two o'clock when Maria was done with her interview. They liked her so much they took her to lunch. Paulie was still at the office. Maria decided to go there after her meeting. When Maria returned, she was very excited. They were so impressed with her resume and where she worked, they hired her on the spot. She would take over the monitoring of the building of the hotel. The staff liked many of Maria's ideas. They fit within the vision and mission of the corporation. Due to her experience, her starting salary was higher than an entry-level salary, which would increase when the hotel opened. Maria had an assistant and many benefits. Along with full medical, she would receive a yearly bonus, a car, and a cell phone. She would be starting after her two-week vacation was over. Maria never owned a car in the city. Paulie and Maria were happy they would not have to spend the money and buy a second car. Since they were engaged, they pooled their money. They had not set a wedding date because they wanted to buy their own house rather than rent. They could stay at the hotel when it opened, but they wanted to feel settled since this would be their first home together. Paulie wanted to pay rent to his parents, but they would not hear of it. As much as they loved him being home, they knew he was going to be getting his own place. They told him to save the money. There were few homes for sale at that time. People did not leave this town. When the one you liked came on the market, someone had to move on it or lose it. It was a great day. There was much good news to share. Paulie and Maria were all settled in. Paulie would spend the next couple of days introducing Maria around town and showing her some of the sights. The next two days passed quickly. Maria helped with some last-minute details for the wedding. It was Friday, and the weather forecast for tomorrow was perfect. Everyone met for lunch Friday afternoon.

Molly was a traditionalist. She told David he could not see the bride the night before the wedding. You, Lou, and the baby can stay at our house. I will stay with Allie. Maria is staying over as well. You will see her in the morning at the church.

David replied, "Really? We have a baby, a house, and live together."

Molly said, "That's it, no exceptions."

Paulie laughed and said, "I'll come and stay with you guys. My mother is driving me crazy. I need a night out."

They all laughed and agreed. Everyone went back to work, and later met for dinner in town. When they all got home, they went to their designated places. Allie and David thought this was crazy, but were happy Molly was excited. That excited them. Everyone had a hard time sleeping. David and Allie ended up packing for their brief trip to Niagara Falls since they decided not to go into the city. They would be returning Thursday. They had decided a trip to Aruba would be perfect for their official honeymoon trip over the colder months.

*****

Their special day finally arrived. It was a perfect day for a wedding. The limo arrived on time to get the girls, and the boys were already at the church. The church was decorated beautifully. The organ was playing as the limo arrived. David had already seen Ray, Russell, and others that were in the church as people were being seated. It was time for everyone to take his or her places.

David leaned over to Paulie and said, "Between you and your sister. I think this is the start of more weddings to come."

Paulie smiled. Julie was engaged. They had not set a date yet, and Paulie had just become engaged. As David and Paulie stood at the altar, the music stopped for a moment. When it started again, the bridal party started to walk slowly down the main aisle. The bridesmaid dresses were beautiful. The material was a light yellow and draped over one shoulder. They were simple, yet elegant. There were three bridesmaids and three groomsmen. Allie asked Lou to give her away. When the bridal party was in place, the music stopped. Allie and Lou turned to face the main aisle. David could now see Allie. She wore a satin finished white gown that draped over each shoulder and ended with short sleeves. She wore a long veil, and her dress filled out from the waist down and boasted a long train. There was also a singer at the church. When the music started, Lou and Allie started their slow walk down the aisle. When they reached the altar, Allie took her place next to David. It was a traditional Catholic wedding with all the trimmings. At the end of the ceremony, most had tears in their eyes. Allie and David along with the bridal party made their way down the aisle and out to the steps of the church to form the reception line.

When everyone left, the wedding party left to take photos while the guests went to the hotel's main ballroom for the cocktail hour. Allie and David would arrive soon. Lou could not help but notice the concerned look on Ray's face. Ray tried very hard to hide it. He and Max had gotten very close over the past five and a half years. He was worried. This was not like Max. He was responsible and solid as a rock. They had a traditional wedding reception with all the trimmings. Most of the people from the town turned out for the wedding.

During the afternoon, Lou approached Ray and said, "Let's go have a cigar."

They went outside, and Lou put it out there. "Have you heard from Max? Your concern is written all over your face."

"No one has. Lou, this is not good. I have enough evidence without his testimony. I have his deposition and statements, as well as notes, recordings, and videos. This is not about that. He is my friend."

Lou said, "I completely understand."

Ray explained, "This is not the day to talk about this."

Lou told him, "Ray. You are my friend. Any day is the day if you need to talk."

Ray explained that Russell was making every effort possible to assist. He was leaving no stone unturned. They were able to track Max's movements until he left for the airport. The trail just stopped. He had already turned in his car and was going to take a cab to the airport. The cab arrived, but Max never came out. They exchanged thoughts, and Ray promised to keep him informed. There was no car to search for, no other trail to follow.

Ray said, "I feel like it's my fault. I tried to have an agent take him to the airport, but Max wouldn't have it."

"Are you ever going to tell me his real name?"

"You know I can't. If Max has chosen to disappear, he's the best. However, he never alluded to that. It wasn't his style."

Lou replied, "The truth will come out. Either the cab driver is lying, something happened, or he may have reconsidered. One day, we will know."

Ray replied, "The FBI team and Russell's team, examined every square inch of his apartment and every way in and out. They did not find a clue. All we can do is hope."

They were quiet for a moment, finished their cigar, and Ray said, "You know, no matter what, the battle rages on." They walked back inside.

At the end of the day, many people were still there. It was a long day. No one was going back to the house. Allie and David were glad that they were packed and ready to leave in the morning. They needed a good night's sleep before they left. The baby was good all day. Molly loved having him with her and everyone crowding around him. He was getting so big. Everyone stayed up talking about how wonderful the day was. Allie and David were going to miss the baby, but they were looking forward to some rest and alone time. Things were busy and stressful for the past few weeks. They needed the break. When they returned, the show was only a few days away. Once that passed, life would return to normal. The two girls Molly and Allie hired were doing great. They were pro's and knew the business. It was simply a matter of adapting to the new designs and visions of the company. Allie and David had decided there would be no business talk while they were away. These four days would be just about them. Sunday morning came, and they headed for the falls. The drive would not be bad. They stopped a couple of times to take photos, and when they got there, they checked into their hotel and just felt relieved.

*****

Meanwhile back home, it was now Monday. Paulie and Maria were settling into living together quite well. They were much like

Allie and David. They were equally independent of each other as they were dependent on one another. Paulie was learning his way around. He was spending time on conference calls and was working on small assignments. He also had to study. He would be required to obtain his investigator's license. Maria spent time at the hotel. Even though she was not on salary until the following next Monday, she had computer training that needed to be done, fill out paperwork, and she wanted to get to know the layout of the hotel and the construction supervisor. Her assistant was handling things temporarily until she took over. Everyone was busy doing his or her thing. David and Allie called every night to check on the baby and let him hear their voices through the phone. They were having a great time and bought something for everyone, and took many pictures. They did and saw as much as they could in four days. They would be leaving Thursday afternoon and would not get in until late Thursday night. Paulie was a natural. Except for the methods, where he came from was not that different. Lou and Russell set up Paulie with access to all the necessary databases they used. Lou was quite impressed as to how quickly he was catching on. Although he was not due to see Clark until next week, he showed him the courtesy of stopping in and keeping him informed. Like he and David, they all grew up together. Clark knew him well. Clark appreciated his enthusiasm and respected him for turning his life around. Paulie changed his appearance. He no longer had slicked-back hair and wore cheesy clothes. Maria helped him with that. He looked like a professional. He was talking about taking on an online college course to get a public service degree. There was no rush. Was it the scare, or Maria that caused this major change? It was probably a combination of both he thought.

It was late Wednesday night when Lou got a call from Russell. By the sound of Russell's voice, Lou could tell something was wrong.

Lou said, "Okay, something is wrong. I could hear it in your voice."

"God Lou; I don't know how to say this."

"Is it, Max?"

Russ replied, "Partially, but worse than that."

Lou said, "Just give it to me and don't sugar coat it."

Russ replied, "We found Max. His body was found this afternoon with a knife through his heart. He was found in an abandoned building by the fire department when they responded to a fire in the Bronx. The fire never reached his body, but he was decomposed. They sent his body to the federal medical examiner's office, not the morgue."

Lou said, "That's terrible. Ray must be a mess."

Russ said, "Ray will be calling you. Do not call him. He asked me to make this call first."

"Why would he do that? Is there something you are not telling me? Let's have it, Russ."

"They ran the prints on the knife, and they were David's. There were no other prints." Lou did not reply. Russ asked, "Lou, are you alright? Are you there?"

"I don't believe it. There has to be more to this. David would never do this. Are they going to arrest him?"

Russ replied, "Ray isn't doing anything yet. He also believes David would not do this. However, so far, the evidence points to David. They placed the time of death sometime between two p.m. and five p.m. the day David was last in the city. Lou, we both know David said he was in his room at that time taking a nap. There is so much here I am going to have to check on. I am sure they will bring him in for questioning. Ray will tell you more as he gets the information. My team is on this along with the FBI forensic team."

Lou said, "Russ, I don't know what to say. We have to wait to see what else is found. Can I count on you?"

Russ replied, "You can always count on me. I believe David did not do this. I only have to prove it. Are you going to be able to handle this?

"Handle it? Are you kidding me? I'm all over it."

Russ replied, "Myself and Ray will handle this. Understand, he may have to do what he needs to do before we get to the truth. We should know more tomorrow."

"Hell Russ, David is a criminal defense attorney, do you think he is that stupid to leave the murder weapon at the murder scene, or in the victim with his prints on it?"

"Lou, I'm not even going to answer that question. We both know the answer. If anyone could commit the perfect crime, David could probably do it with the knowledge he has. There is much more to this. Trust me. We will find the underlying cause of it. It can't be any harder than what we had to do with Allie's case, and look how we did on that."

Lou replied, "I'm sorry. It's upsetting because I don't know how I'm going to tell Molly."

Russ said, "It's simple. Don't, not yet. It will take days or weeks before we know all the facts, and all the forensic evidence is examined and evaluated. Ray will not be talking to David until after Allie's show. There is not enough information yet. Stay calm. You know I will be all over this."

"It's always something. When will these kids get a break?"

Russ said, "Keep the faith and never lose the family trust. The last thing we need is the family falling apart. I'm glad Paulie is out. I may need his help on this one."

They hung up, but Lou could not sleep. He kept thinking how he was going to hide this from Molly for now. He knew at some point when David was picked up for questioning he would have to tell her before that happened. He thought for a minute and then placed a call to Ray. He got his voice mail. Lou said, "Ray, it's Lou. Russell and I just got off the phone. You don't have to call me back. I know it's late. I'm sure you know that along with your people, Russell and I will be quite involved. We have worked together before, and we can do it again. I want you to know that I respect whatever you will need to do. You know David did not do this, and he is not going to run. As a favor to me, I have not said anything to Molly yet. When the time comes, please give me a few days to tell her and prepare her. If I tell her now, she will be a wreck. I prefer that time to be as short as possible. Thank you."

Ray called Lou right back. They were friends, and he knew how Lou was feeling. When Lou answered Ray said, "Hi. Thank you for understanding. Lou, you know I do not believe that David did this, even though all the evidence so far points to him. We all know from Allie's case that the evidence is always not as clear-cut as it looks. David will get the benefit of the doubt, but you know the process I will have to follow. Russell and my team will be working on this together. I only asked Russell to call because I had a meeting, and honestly my friend, I did not know what to say. I will certainly give you time when the time comes to prepare Molly and Allie. I know David isn't going anywhere."

Lou thanked him and said, "Get some sleep and thanks for calling me back. Together, we will get to the truth. We did it once, we can do it again."

Molly was asleep, and Lou was in the den with the door closed. Molly had never seen him shed one tear until the baby was born, and at the wedding. He did not want her to see them now. He finally went to bed and fell asleep. Tomorrow will come soon enough. He was going to have to be a good actor. Since nothing would happen until after the fashion show, he decided not even to tell David until after the show. Could he do this?

CHAPTER 7

EVERYTHING HAS A PROCESS

It was Thursday, and Paulie stopped by the office. Lou told him everything and swore him to secrecy. Paulie already spoke with Russell. Russell explained where he might be able to help when the time came. Paulie swore he would not say a word to anyone.

Lou explained, "This is the life we chose. We must understand we cannot discuss our business outside of this office with anyone, and sometimes, not even our family."

Paulie replied, "I understand. You can trust me. Between all of us, we will find out the truth."

"Yes, we will. We are the ones that are going to have to be strong now. Are you up to this?"

Paulie replied, "Without a doubt."

The rest of the day was uneventful. Lou was worried, which was not like him, but he could not help it. Having so many things going through his mind, he knew he had to get control of himself. When David and Allie got back that evening, Paulie and Maria were visiting. They gave everyone their gifts and started showing them the pictures of everything they had done. The fashion show was this weekend. Everything was ready. Paulie and Lou did an excellent job of hiding their emotions. For a while, they were not even thinking about all that was going on. It was late, and everyone went to bed.

The next day David was off from work and helping Allie. Lou was in the office. It did not take Russell long to go to work. As priorities go, this was number one on the list. Russell had many people working on other cases. They knew what they were doing. Russell pulled in two of his best people. One would assist with the forensic autopsy, and the other would start doing investigating work in the city. There was much to do. They started canvassing the area, putting together the surrounding video camera footage for a six-block radius around David's hotel the day he was in the city. They wanted to try to retrace his steps and timestamp everything in any video where David appeared. Besides what the government used, Russell had some of the most advanced facial recognition software available. In these cases, the timeline is critical. It could make or break an investigation. The big problem was David did not have an alibi between 1:30 p.m. and five p.m. until Paulie called. Even when Paulie called, he called David's cell phone, not his room, so in reality, David would not be able to account for his time until 6:30 p.m. when he met Paulie for dinner. He was in his hotel room alone. That made for plenty of time to commit the murder, drop the body in the Bronx, and get back to the hotel. Ray sent Russell the warrants for these items. The FBI had not impounded David's car yet. They knew that would be coming soon. Ray and Russ needed to get David's car. If you remember, he left it in the hotel lot the entire time and used cab services to get around. How will an FBI forensic agent and one of Russell's team check David's car without David knowing it? They decided to wait until after the fashion show. That is when Lou was planning to break the news to David. He hoped this would all work out. Meanwhile, Russell's agent in the city was going to spend that entire weekend getting as much surveillance video as possible.

On Saturday, they spend the morning getting ready to meet guests as they arrived. Allie had received some last minute responses and found she would have TV coverage of her show. She was the 'new guy on the block.' Everyone was curious. Reporters and crews from three major networks would be there. The event would begin at 6 p.m. Camera crews, and guests started arriving around one o'clock. Nothing was forgotten, and no stone was left unturned. Allie and Molly were getting ready to produce one of the more elegant fashion shows in the industry. Although Lou never told her, he was quite instrumental in getting her the news coverage. The adrenaline and excitement were flowing. It was now six, and the festivities began. As their staff was handling everything behind the scenes, Allie and Molly were in the audience networking. It was a full house and standing room only. It was going perfectly. Allie and Molly looked elegant. Lou and David were in tuxedos and gave the girls the space they needed to network. They posted no pictures of the line. Allie and Molly wanted this to be a complete surprise. They had a piano player during the cocktail hour and a DJ for when the actual show began. He was a pro at this. He analyzed the line and chose the proper music, which Allie and Molly approved. As with most events, the actual show started a bit late, which was fine. When the lights dimmed, the show started. The music and visual effects in the background were outstanding. Every model looked perfect. Allie and Molly could not have been happier. There was a break between the fall and winter line to give people time to stretch their legs, have a cocktail and chat. This also gave the model's time to freshen up their makeup, relax, and get ready for the next line. There were three hairdressers, three makeup professionals, and a tailor in the dressing rooms. Molly did want the models to be under stress. It was paramount that they focus on what they were there to do.

The first half was flawless. The compliments and chatter they overheard were all positive. After the second half was over, they received a standing ovation. The models came back out on stage for a bow. The DJ was hired to stay and play dance music for those who wanted to dance. The stage was pulled back to make room and set up the buffet. The piano player was playing in the smaller room for those who wanted a quieter atmosphere. They had a table set up to take orders from anyone who wanted to place one. There was food in both rooms and open bar all night. This night costs them a fortune. Anyone staying overnight had complimentary rooms. Allie and Molly would greet them in the morning, and provide a continental breakfast. Everything ended around midnight. It turned out that both girls they hired, Candee and Melissa, had been taking orders most of the evening. Everyone was buying the line. When they looked at the figures at 11:30, they were astonished. They had received over two million dollars in orders. Once the word got around, they would receive more. The event was a complete success. Allie and Molly were interviewed on television. One of the fashion reporters stated, "I have been to shows all over the world. This is the first show I have ever attended that combined style, grace, and a comfortable atmosphere." The owners of the Allie M. fashion line would soon be the talk of the fashion industry once all the articles and news reviews were published. Two of the largest clothing distributors who attended were expecting large orders from their smaller shops. Allie and Molly gave birth to a new chapter in their lives. That night belonged to Allie and Molly. Lou was very busy throughout the night. He had not given much thought about what he would soon have to tell David. He was wondering if he should do it as a family, or just the two of them alone. He knew it had to be soon. He thought talking as a family would be best. Everyone could support one another. Russell and the FBI techs wanted to get David's car by Tuesday. This did not give Lou much time. He did not want to spoil this moment. He knew they would be on cloud nine for days. However, Lou did not have days. Lou decided to talk to the family Sunday evening. A talk he was not looking forward to having.

It was Sunday morning, and the continental breakfast was excellent. Everyone who had stayed the night would be gone by eleven a.m. Even though everyone was tired, they attended late mass. When they returned home, they all took a nap. Thankfully, the baby slept the whole time. Lou was feeling quite anxious when he awoke. It was around four o'clock, and he thought there was no time like the present. He told everyone they needed to have a family meeting. He was not sure how to start, so he thought it best to get right to the point. He knew this would be quite emotional. His goal was to keep everyone calm. He had a conference call with Ray and Russell on Monday. They wanted David on it as well. The plan was to take David's car on Tuesday. He knew David would want to represent himself, but Lou was not sure if that was the best idea. He had an excellent criminal defense attorney he used in the past and thought that might be the best way to go. He thought David would not have it. Another issue they would have to discuss on Monday. There were many unknowns and many decisions to make. There was so much evidence still yet to be found and analyzed before they would know exactly how things would shape up. He also was concerned about whether or not Ray could remain unbiased. He and Max were very close. His gut feeling was Ray could. Ray was a professional. Ray always searched for the truth, and never took the easy way out. Lou had looked at this from many angles, although he knew David did not kill Max because it would serve no purpose. Lou firmly believed David was set up, probably as revenge from Vincent since David would not represent him. The key would be if they could unfold that mystery.

It was time. Everyone was at the table and still talking about the previous night. Their spirits were high. Lou said, "I have some startling news we all need to discuss. I wanted to wait until after the show not to spoil that moment. However, it can't wait any longer."

David said, "Let's have it, dad. What's up?"

"David, Max's body turned up. He is dead. The time of death goes back to the time you were in the city during the hours you were napping. They found him with a knife in his chest. The knife had your fingerprints on it."

David exclaimed, "WHAT? How could that be?" Then David thought and said, "Dad, remember the guy that followed me and came up behind my car? He saw me with my knife pulling the piece of glass out of my tire. They must have gotten into my car while it was parked in the hotel garage. They removed my knife and used it to kill Max. After the arrests, they knew Max was an informant and FBI agent. They left the knife to set me up for the murder. Let me go check my car to see if the knife is there."

Lou and David went to the car. They wore gloves, opened the trunk, and the knife was gone. They had the start of a theory, which would depend on what the other evidence revealed.

Lou and David went back inside. Allie and Molly were a wreck crying. David said, "Stop crying. We all need to be strong. We will get to the bottom of this." He asked Lou, "What were Ray's intentions?"

"For now, he had none. He will have to question you. He said he would come here for that. They are taking your car on Tuesday for a full forensic work up. Dave, Russell is already on this pulling surveillance video for every camera in the hotel, and all they could find in a six-block radius around your hotel. Ray's team and Russell will be working together. Ray assured me he would make no arrests at this time. The investigation just started. However, since Max was an agent, he is under a great deal of pressure from above."

"Can we trust Ray? After all, they were close friends. Can he be objective?"

Lou replied, "I believe we can, and so does Russell. However, be prepared for the worst."

Allie took his hand, "Babe, I'm right here and never leaving your side. Let the people who love you handle this."

Lou said, "I was going to wait until tomorrow to ask you. We have a conference call with Ray and Russ at ten in the morning. Do you think we should get Palmer and Sons to represent you? Besides you, they are the best in the business."

David shocked Lou with his answer since Lou thought David would be against it. David said, "Yes, under one condition."

Lou asked, "What's that."

"I will work side by side with them. They will only take control if something more drastic happens. Dad, no one can defend me better than I can, but in this case, it makes sense to have help."

Lou, Allie, and Molly agreed. They were happy that David was thinking sensibly about this. Everyone was very upset. It was like reliving the past all over again. Would life ever be normal? Now, it was just a waiting game. Everyone went to bed. The next weeks would be quite stressful.

On Monday, when David and Lou got to the office, Lou called Palmer and Sons. He knew the firm's owner very well. Lou explained the situation. Mike, the lead attorney, heard all the rumbles about all the arrests. It was big news. He was perfectly willing to join the legal team at no charge, informing them it was professional courtesy. He knew that they would do the same and had in the past with personal real estate investments. He wanted to be part of the conference call scheduled for ten o'clock. He knew Ray very well since they had many cases together. His son and David attended the same law school. Everyone knew one another, which made it much easier. It was about nine-thirty, and Russell called. He wanted to speak with Lou before the conference call. Lou told him the family knew. Russell thought that was good and said, "Let's get Dave on the phone."

When the three were on the phone, Russell explained his people were still collecting surveillance video. That is a large undertaking. It will take time to review. Some systems only save their videos for twenty-four hours, and this was over a week ago. He explained the full forensic autopsy on Max was starting today, and they would get David's car tomorrow. Russell was still trying to create some form of a timeline on Max's day. They chatted back and forth with some ideas when Lou's private line rang, and it was Ray.

Ray, Russell, Lou, David, and Michael Palmer from Palmer and Sons were all on the call. Everyone knew each other so it would be a comfortable call. No one would be making accusations. Ray started the conversation by explaining that they all needed to state what they knew, and discuss those items as they went ago. Everyone needed to be transparent. He told them everyone at the bureau knew David. No one thought for a minute, David committed this crime. He further explained, for the moment, he would still be referring to the deceased as Max.

Michael Palmer interjected and said, "Ray, at some point we need to know his real identity. As much as I appreciate that no one believes David did this, we are going to have to do our due diligence."

Ray explained he understood. The problem is he was getting a new identity. He asked their understanding since so many cases depend on this. Everyone understood and respected that. Not just for Max, but for whatever family he may still have left. Security now was paramount. Especially now with all these other cases in progress. Ray explained there was a great deal of pressure from above to find out who did this since Max was an agent. Ray started it off and asked for a moment to go over the next set of events that would happen.

Ray started by explaining that between the new baby, the wedding, and the fashion show, this was the last thing anyone expected. Ray added, "Let me tell you what we have so far, which isn't much."

Ray said, "We all know Max's body was found with a knife through his heart. It had David's fingerprints on it. Yours were the only prints that we found on the knife. However, we found other particulates on the knife. Russ and the FBI team were trying to identify what they were, and where they might have originated. The autopsy on Max was starting today. It would be a slow process. One of Russell's forensic coroners is also on the autopsy team. Dave, tomorrow Russ and I are sending a team to get your car. We are going to bring it back to our lab. I am sure you understand we have to go through it thoroughly. Let me ask everyone a question. How would you feel if I came down tomorrow with our stenographer and took David's statement and asked him some questions?"

No one thought that was a problem. Everyone would all be there.

Lou asked, "Do you want to use my private conference room since it's soundproof and secure?"

"That would be great. As I said earlier, I am under a great deal of pressure on this one, but I will not jump to any conclusions, we will find out the truth."

They decided to meet at 10 a.m. Ray wanted everyone to feel comfortable. This was the first of many steps to come. They ended their call, and those remaining stayed on the phone to continue the discussion.

Mike Palmer stated, "Gentleman, I know we all know Ray. However, he has a job to do. We all trust him, but let's not rely too much on that. When push comes to shove, he will have to do his job. He is not the one pulling strings here. He will be watched closely on this and will be under a great deal of pressure to find out what happened. Let's not forget that."

Everyone agreed. David said, "I want us to be truthful and cooperative. I know I did not do this. However, no one knows how deep this goes, and who may be involved. I think it is best for them to show their hand as we move forward. Russ, how much more footage does your team estimate we will get, and how long will it take."

"My people informed me they should have more on Wednesday. They are getting as much as they can. The biggest problem we are facing is that due to cost, many businesses only keep video storage for twenty-four hours. There may be things we could have seen that may not be available."

David replied, "We will cross each bridge as we come to it."

Meanwhile, Jeff, the Chief of Police stopped in to see Lou. He entered the conference room and asked, "What the hell is going on?" The FBI just had me seal David's car until they arrive tomorrow. Does someone want to fill me in?"

Lou said, "Have a seat, and I will summarize it for you. You should probably be aware of this."

Jeff sat down so Lou could brief him. Jeff replied, "This is crazy, David would never do that, this is a frame up. Thanks for filling me in and please keep me in the loop. I will assist any way I can."

Everyone thanked him. He left. There was not much left to do now until they started to get more information and correlated it. David and Lou tried not to worry about this and went back to their day. Business still had to continue. Allie called and asked David how it went. He made sure to sound confident so she would not worry. He explained everything they discussed. David was not worried, but concerned. He knows how evidence can be deceiving, and how a frame-up can end up with an innocent person going to jail. Take Allie's case as an example. It happens. He knew he could not let this consume him. He had a full caseload that also needed his attention. Paulie was getting involved with Russell to help him on this. Paulie had connections with those that were involved back in the city. He did not know if they were high enough up to get any answers, and they certainly needed to be careful if they tried. Paulie and Russell were working out a strategy for trying this approach. Ray knew about it and was very willing to work with anyone who could provide information on this. It takes a lot of balls to murder a federal agent. Anyone who does that must know the heat will be tremendous.

Ray started putting more pressure on those that were not arrested in the initial sting. Even the city police were clamping down. There was a raid somewhere almost every night. Prostitutes were brought in for questioning and were arrested for soliciting. It was not business as usual. These people used to get a pass because they often gave the police good information. One hand washed the other. In this case, everyone was scared to death. No one would say a word. Was that because they did not know anything? Could David have murdered Max? Ray did not believe that for a moment. The one thing that was lacking at this time was a motive. What motive could David have to kill Max? Did it have something to do with an old grudge from the days past? David never knew Max was an FBI agent who had been undercover in the family for over five years. Ray would continue to squeeze everyone until someone finally cracked. He vowed to find out the truth, even if David was involved. It had escalated a point that whatever prostitution or gambling still going on was either in new locations or suffering even more. The downside was; the authorities were also not getting information on anything else. Ray was willing to take this tradeoff to find Max's killer.

*****

It was now Monday night. David rented a car because he did not have access to his and needed to get around. He did not want Charlie, the firm's driver, to have to drive him everywhere he needed to be. Russell called the house and spoke to Lou and David. He did not have good news. When they removed the knife from Max's chest, there was evidence of small particulates in the wound, which were swabbed and removed for further testing. The team determined Max was murdered somewhere else and moved to that building. The fire was deliberately set. The interesting part is, the room that Max's body was in was not the room where the fire was started. Whoever put the body in that room, wanted it to be found. It was probably a message, and to frame David. They checked all the surrounding areas. They did not discover any additional evidence. The fire never got to the room where Max's body was placed. The room was intact. Max had to be killed somewhere else and placed there. They were examining his clothing, shoes, and anything they could to attempt to determine where the actual murder took place. The types of maggots found on the body narrowed down the time of death. The bad news being, after they removed the knife, they found a piece of fiber, and hair in the wound. They ran a DNA match on the hair, and it belonged to David. They would compare the fibers when they took possession of David's car. If they were also a match, the evidence would be piling up. When the firefighters found Max's body, he was in a plastic bag that had been eaten through by rodents. They were checking everything.

David said, "None of this concerns me. Since the knife was mine, and I was recently using it on the tire, a piece of my hair or trunk fiber could have gotten on it. I can easily dispute this evidence. The most important thing they are missing is a motive. They have to show motive as well as opportunity and produce irrefutable evidence. They have none of that so far. At best, they have what could be considered a theory. They have so much yet to find. They need to know where the actual murder took place. Then they have to be able to place me at the crime scene. Even with that, they need a motive. Tomorrow's questioning would be interesting."

Russell replied, "Don't shoot the messenger, but let's not forget. I am assisting here, and do not have access to everything they may or may not know. Your biggest issue is you were alone napping. You have no alibi, and the hotel only saves their surveillance videos for seven days, so we do not have that as a reference. I have requested your cell phone records with details. Maybe we can see which cell tower your calls went through during that timeframe since you spoke with Paulie. I don't expect that will be much help, but I want to cover all the bases. I was hoping for garage video footage. That would help to show if someone tampered with your car. We are hoping we will find that out when we get your car into the lab. I will not lie to you. We have a great deal of camera footage to review. Ray is very helpful. He is going to allow us to use their facial recognition software to compare all the footage to your face, Max, other known people in the organization, as well as who might be in their database. If there is anything to find, I will find it. I have my people also asking around through their connections. I want to use Paulie as a last resort due to his parole restrictions. I would need permission from his parole officer to get him involved, which I don't believe Clark would object."

David and Lou both thanked him for doing such excellent work. Russell said, "Listen to me guys. You are both to close to this. One stupid thing you say or do can hurt us. Dave, let me and Michael handle this. It's great for you to confer with him and assist him with your experience, but let him be your attorney."

David replied, "Yes Russ. I know you're right."

Lou added, "Don't worry; I'll keep David in line."

David told Lou he was feeling good about this. Lou said, "Dave, I want to see this resolved. You know better than I do that this has just begun. This is still round one. If Vincent had a part of this, which I'm sure he did, you could be sure he has other things lined up to make it look like you did it. He didn't get to the top of the food chain because he's stupid."

David replied, "I know. However, we have the best in the business working with us. What we accomplished for Allie, no one else in this world could do. The ride might get rough, but I know we will win in the end."

The girls just sat back and listened. They knew if the boys wanted their advice, they would ask for it. They knew this would be like taking three steps forward and two steps backward. They already accepted that at some point, David might be charged with the crime. However, they knew what this team was capable of accomplishing. They had total faith in them. Regardless of how tough it was. They knew they needed to stay strong for Lou and David. Regardless of what happened. They were tough women. They always said, "Don't let our looks fool you." That night you could feel the tension in the air. No one talked much.

Molly finally broke the silence and said, "Look. We cannot live like this until this gets resolved. We have to go on with our lives like we always do."

Everyone agreed and started talking, which made everyone feel more relaxed. When everyone awoke in the morning, Lou wanted to create a relaxed atmosphere. He had a variety of breakfast items and coffee at the office. Ray, the stenographer, Russell, and Mike Palmer arrived around 9:15. They were early. Lou and David were there. They arrived at the office early. The FBI team came to take David's car to their lab. Everyone sat down and ate breakfast. Ray started the dialog. He explained this was an informal proceeding for fact-finding purposes. Mike Palmer, David's attorney, explained that he did not intend to advise David not to answer all questions. They wanted to cooperate and be completely transparent. He made it quite clear that he has not been made aware through full disclosure of all the facts the FBI had found. He may have to advise his client not to answer a question that pertained to anything that had not yet been disclosed.

Ray said, "I understand. I want this to be comfortable and relaxed. The government is not making any accusations at this time. I'm only trying to piece together a timeline." They all agreed, and it started.

Ray asked David to explain the events of that day. David explained he drove into town for Paulie's sentencing hearing. He and Ray had spoken the night before regarding the hearing. He and Ray met at the courthouse at nine a.m. the following morning. He went to court at ten a.m. to wrap that up. He and Paulie decided to meet for dinner later that evening. He was going to call me later that day so we could arrange a time to meet. I decided to see one of our clients and have lunch with them. David handed Ray the lunch receipt, which was time-stamped and dated. Lunch was over about one o'clock. David called Lou to update him and decided to shop for a gift for Molly and Allie. He gave those receipts to Ray. They were also time stamped and dated. David got back to the hotel at two-thirty. He explained he was tired and decided to take a nap. Paulie called around five-thirty, which woke David up. They decided to meet at the hotel restaurant at six-thirty. David explained he got up, showered, and changed. He met Paulie for dinner at six-thirty. After dinner, Paulie went back to his room, and after calling home, they went to sleep. David explained that Paulie stayed over because they had to meet with his parole officer early the next day, and wanted to get up early to have breakfast first. David gave Ray the phone company records revealing the time Paulie called. We met with his parole officer, and I went back to my hotel. I never went back to my room. The valet attendant got my car, and I left. I also spoke to Allie and Lou that night which is listed on my cell phone records.

Ray asked, "So no one saw you between two- thirty and five-thirty that afternoon?"

"No. I was napping in my room and alone.

Ray asked, "Tell me about your fishing knife."

David replied, "I haven't fished in years, but I always kept the knife in my toolbox, which is always in the trunk of my car. I have not used that knife in a long time until I used it to pry the piece of glass out of the tire. I kept it handy when the unidentified man approached the trunk of my car. The tire was already in the trunk.

I am sure he saw the knife. I was holding it in my hand. After he left, I placed the tire flat. It slipped and hit my hand causing me to drop the knife, which stuck in the carpet. I removed it, put it back in the toolbox, and went on my way."

Ray asked, "Have you ever met Max?"

"Yes. A little over two years ago, I was going to the parties when I worked in New York. The firm I worked for had them as clients."

Ray asked, "Did you and Max ever have any problems with each other, fights, arguments, or anything of that nature?"

"No."

Ray asked, "Was Max the person who approached you? Did he hint at threatening you and Paulie if you didn't help retrieve the ledger?"

Michael Palmer interjected and said, "David, don't answer that question. Ray, if you had this information before, explain why you never mentioned this to my client or Lou during your past dealings together? What type of game are you playing here? Besides, the answer to that question is irrelevant since those events are in the past. My client was not arrested nor convicted of any crime. Also, at your request, David called Max to set up a meeting with Vincent. I would think if they had any issues, David would have never made that call."

Ray replied, "I disagree. It could speak to a possible motive."

David said, "Mike, let me answer the question. Ray, Max was someone doing his job. Paulie and I got ourselves into that mess. That was not Max's fault. I had, nor do I have any issues with him."

Ray said, "What if I told you we have a witness who stated they witnessed you and Max having an argument the day he was killed."

"I guess I would have to say you don't have a witness; you have a liar."

Michael stood up and said, "This interview is over. Although we are not in a court of law, the rules of discovery are not only law they are a courtesy. I will not allow my client to answer any further question without having knowledge of the evidence you claim you have. I emphasize, claim to have in evidence since I have seen nothing regarding this."

Ray responded, "Mike. David is not under arrest, nor do I plan to do that at this time. This is just a fact-finding meeting. However, if you are going to walk out with your client, you will force me to take David into custody, and I can ask these questions later. If you still refuse to have him answer them when I arrest him, he could be charged with obstruction. Is this really what you want, or should we all calm down?"

Mike replied, "Of course I don't want that, and neither does David. Rather than try to trick us. Let's all calm down and be upfront about what we all know."

Everyone agreed that it was getting out of hand and understood the pressure Ray was under from his boss to find Max's killer.

Lou said, "Ray, we all go back a long time. Without us, you would not have the opportunities you have today. If you are telling us the truth, and you do not believe David committed this crime, take the emotions out of it. David will answer everything, but he will not be tricked. Neither Mike nor I will allow that. We all know you can take him into custody for questioning. We all know you do not have enough evidence to charge him. The most you can do is hold him for twenty-four hours. After that, if you charge him, I will request that the judge order his release. Do any of us want to walk down that path?"

Ray informed the stenographer to strike all of that from the record. "I'm sorry. There is so much going on. The brass are breathing down my neck every day."

Lou replied, "If everyone agrees, let's continue." Everyone agreed.

David said, "Ray, I don't know who your witness is, or who they are tied to. I am sure you are looking into that. All I can say is, I held no mal-intent towards Max. I did not murder him. I do not even know where he lived. I never saw or argued with him that day. You are aware of the only two times I spoke with him, from me, and probably from him. After all, he was your agent."

Ray replied, "Fair enough. We are looking into it. Dave, do you have any idea why you might think you are being framed."

"Isn't it obvious? Vincent wanted me to defend him, and I refused. Paulie would testify that people were talking about Vincent trying to get me on board, and the man who approached me said it was a message." Vincent was pissed I would not defend him. Vincent does not like being told no. You know all of this is true because you helped set the trap to get me out of helping him and get Paulie off the hook. Ray replied, "I do not have any further questions at this time. However, I am sure you understand I may need to meet with you again. Dave, please understand. The time may come where I have to do something I really don't want to do."

"I know you have a job to do, and no one knows how deep this may go. I only ask one thing. If things take a turn that requires you to have to arrest me, do not keep me in jail. Make it a house arrest. I will wear an ankle bracelet. You know Ray, one way or another, Russell and this family will find the truth."

Ray replied, "I will try. That may not be my decision. If I cannot arrange that, I may be able to have you held locally. Let's hope it doesn't come to that."

For the moment, the interview was over. Ray and the stenographer left, and David's car was taken to the lab. Everyone else stayed behind. David said, "Listen, everyone, I'm telling you now, this is going to wind up in an arrest." Russell agreed.

David went on to say, "The fibers they found in the wound Max sustained are going to match the carpet in my trunk. That knife was taken from my trunk. It must have been taken sometime during my stay in the city. I told Ray the knife stuck into the carpet. I think that will prove out. It is my knife. Therefore, my fingerprints would be on it.

Furthermore, I have no alibi. The FBI claims to have a witness who states they saw me arguing with Max that day. I'm sure it's probably some bimbo Vincent is paying."

Russell interrupted and said, "Dave, we ran a check on her. She is a secretary who works in an office downtown. She is a mother and has been married for ten years. She has no criminal record. Ray hasn't seen that yet."

"I don't give a damn who she is. Somehow, she has a connection to Vincent."

Russell replied, "I agree. We are getting everything on her from the day she was born. Tax records, medical records, everything. If she has any ties to Vincent, we will find it."

Dave said, "Dad, once Ray gets all this information, he won't have any other choice but to arrest me. Whether he wants to or not. His boss will give him no choice. The evidence is piling up."

Lou replied, "Let us worry about that. Russ, make sure your people do not miss anything on David's car. No one can hide everything. Somewhere we will find the opening."

Russell replied, "Don't worry Lou. This ball game is far from over."

Lunch was delivered, and they had a bite to eat. David got up and told everyone he was going over to talk to Allie. He knew what was going to happen next. Lou thought they should wait and talk to the girls together at dinner tonight. Why upset their day? Russell offered to stay the rest of the afternoon and be with them when they told the girls. Maybe the girls hearing some facts and progress from him might help them not to worry as much. Russell's wife came to town with him to see the baby. She was at the shop with the girls. Lou and David didn't know Russell's wife was in town. They insisted they stay for dinner. Lou and David had some work they needed to get done, and Russell wanted to talk with his people. Russell worked out of the conference room while David and Lou wrapped up some miscellaneous things. When Russell was done, he told them he and Paulie were taking a walk over to see the baby. He wanted to chat with Paulie about a couple of ideas he had. They decided to meet at "The Tavern" at six o'clock. It was already four-thirty.

CHAPTER 8

DO YOU KNOW
YOUR RIGHTS?

At six, everyone met at "The Tavern." Besides that fact that it was nice for everyone to be together, it was the perfect time to bring the girls up to speed. Lou called and made a reservation. Since there would be eight people, he wanted a private area reserved. Everyone talked and caught up. The baby slept through most of the dinner. While having coffee, they informed Molly and Allie of all the recent events. Nothing was hidden. David even stated that he felt this would lead to an arrest, telling them this was going to get worse before it got better. However, no one was giving up.

David said, "We all know how close we are to Ray, but try to remember he has people to report to and a job to do. Whether he likes it or not, I am convinced. He will have to arrest me. Please, no one give him a difficult time over this when it happens."

Allie asked, "Babe, do you really think you are going to get arrested?"

David replied, "Yes, and probably by the end of the week."

Allie said, "OH MY GOD," and a tear started to run down her face.

Russell chimed in saying, "I have my best people on this. Vincent may be smart and think he has gotten David, but we are smarter. Somewhere there will be a missing piece, and we will find it. Everyone needs to stay strong and confident no matter how bad this gets. As it stands now, once they take samples of David's trunk, they will have enough evidence to arrest him, and possibly even go to trial. Unless we turn something up, he could be convicted. The one thing we have in our favor is that Ray believes David did not do this. That will give us the time we need to get to the truth."

Everyone felt a little better after hearing those words of reassurance. However, Russell and his team were going to have their hands full working this case. David was both right and wrong. He was right that he would probably be arrested. He was wrong that it would take until the end of the week. Two days later, he received a call from Mike Palmer, his attorney. Mike informed him that Ray had called. A warrant was issued for David's arrest for the murder of Max. Ray informed Mike to have David turn himself in by the end of the day tomorrow. He will get processed and have to stay the night. I still believe David is innocent. When we go to court the next day, I will not hold him and allow him to post bail, so he is home for the weekend. I will continue to work with Russell."

Mike thanked him and said, "We will be there by tomorrow afternoon."

Mike immediately called David, Lou, and Russell, and informed them of this. Lou was furious. Russell was shocked it happened so quickly. David was not surprised. David and Mike decided how to handle the following day. Charlie would drive them and stay the night. This way, he could bring them back the following day after court. Lou had to be in court the next day and could not go. He trusted Ray and expected everything would go as planned. David insisted that Lou not go. Lou was too mad and upset. David felt he should stay close to the girls for support. As much as Lou did not like that idea, he agreed that it was the best course of action. Luckily, they did not have to go into the city. David could go to a closer field office to do this where there was also a federal court. Mike called Ray back to confirm the arrangements. Ray was thankful. It was difficult enough to have to make that call.

On Wednesday morning, David went into the office to get a couple of things done and meet with the other attorneys regarding other cases. Allie and Molly did not go to the shop. Lou was still home with them. David got back to the house around eleven, and Charlie was waiting. Mike was going to drive himself since they would have to go out of their way to pick him up. Allie was in tears and did not want to let go of David. Molly was a wreck, and Lou had all he could do to keep himself together. He had to for the sake of the girls. Paulie was also at the house. He told David he would not sleep until they got him cleared. David was also upset, but he did not want to show it. He held and kissed the baby for a few minutes, then they had to leave.

Charlie said, "Don't worry. I'll take care of him."

David hugged everyone, even Lou. Lou laughed and asked, "What was that all about?" David just replied, "I love you dad." They all walked out to the limo and watched as David drove away with Charlie.

Allie said, "He's not coming back."

Lou replied, "Don't be silly. This is all arranged."

Allie said, "He's not coming back. I just feel it, and he knows it. That's why he hugged you dad. He has never done that. I know my husband, and I know what can happen in the system. I've been there."

Lou replied, "You're just upset. Everything will be fine. He'll be home tomorrow."

It was a nice day. David and Charlie had a nice ride. They talked on the way to the FBI office. Although Charlie never asked questions, he was around enough to know what was going on. He could do the math. Back home, Russell was on the phone with Lou. He was telling Lou that Paulie had stayed up almost all night reviewing surveillance video with his team. Many shop owners only saved their footage for 24 to 48 hours. They did not find anything useful that could help David. The ATM and traffic cam videos were saved for a longer length of time. They were about halfway through them. Russell commented that he was surprised that the hotel did not save theirs for a longer period, especially due to the high amount of car thefts from their garages. Many people drove in and kept their cars there for up to a week at a time.

He told Lou he was sending a man back to the hotel tomorrow. When they first went there, the manager was away. The clerk gave them the videos. It's possible the manager has more stored in his office?"

Lou thought that was a long shot, but worth a try. Lou asked, "Do we know where David's car was parked in the garage?"

Russell replied, "I'm not sure. David probably had the parking attendant park the car for him. Tomorrow I will call the parking manager. Maybe we can catch a break."

They decided to talk again tomorrow. When Lou got home, no one was hungry. No one wanted to eat. Allie just sat quietly holding the bay, and Molly was sitting next to her. No one was talking. For the first time in Lou's life, he did not know what to do. He felt the same way but had to break this mood.

With a semi-stern voice, Lou said, "Let's stop this behavior right now. Is this what you think David wants us all to do? By God, I am not going to see this family fall apart again. I'm just not. Not only do we have David to think about, but we also have my grandson to consider. This is NOT what he is used to. Snap out of this and give me the baby and let's have some dinner."

Almost as if were planned, both Allie and Molly got up. Allie handed the baby to Lou. Allie and Molly gave him a kiss on the cheek and at the same time said, "You're right. What does everyone feel like eating?"

Lou laughed and said, "Anything, as long as I do not have to drive back into town to pick it up."

The girls replied, "Let's finish all those leftovers from the other night."

No one had any idea how complicated things were about to get. Every ounce of strength and love that this family shared would soon be put to the test. Later that night Ray called. The background check on the witness who claimed to see Max and David arguing that day came back clean. He explained the only thing the FBI did not know was where Max was murdered. They also do not have any evidence that David was in the room where Max was found. They were still checking the room and building. After they got off the phone, Lou knew that if they were framing David for this, those things would be discovered. The FBI would find something. Lou called Russell and told him about the conversation.

Russell replied, "Sorry Lou. I don't buy it. There is something about this girl, and I will find it. I just feel it."

Lou replied, "I hope so."

Russell said, "Keep the faith. We will figure it out. Trust me."

It was much later when David called and told everyone that everything was fine. He would call them when court adjourned in the morning. Before they went to work the next day, they wanted to wait until they heard from David. It was late, and everyone was tired due to all the stress. Lou told Allie to stay at their house. They would be all together in the morning when David called. Everyone was up early and ate breakfast. They could not wait to hear from David. They did not know when David went to court Ray was there. There was also another prosecutor with him. Neither Mike nor David liked this. Before court started, Mike went over to Ray.

Mike asked, "What the hell is going on here?"

Ray replied, "I was just taken off this case ten minutes ago. My boss feels because we are all friends, I am too close to it. He didn't want any suspicions or questions asked later."

Mike asked, "I assume the deal is still the same?"

Ray replied, "Honestly, I don't know if this new prosecutor changed anything. I explained what we had discussed. I never met this prosecutor before. I don't know him. I've only heard he can be tough."

Mike replied, "Ray. This is going to piss off a lot of people if this doesn't go as we discussed."

Ray replied, "Mike. You knew he was getting arrested."

"That's not what I'm referring to. I am referring to David not being held and allowed to make bail. We're talking about David here, not some criminal."

Ray replied, "Mike, I've been trying to tell you that the brass is all over this. Max was an agent who was murdered. They want answers and someone's head on a platter."

Mike said, "What about the truth and justice? We don't think about that anymore?"

Mike threw his hands in the air and walked away. He had to let David know before the court was called to order. Mike informed David and was quite surprised by his response. This did not seem to affect him.

Mike asked, "What's up Dave? I thought you would be upset?"

David replied, "Not at all. I thought this might happen. Think about it Mike, it makes sense. I'll bet you we have a different judge as well."

At that moment, the court was instructed to rise. The judge walked in. It was a different judge than they expected. David just looked at Mike. Mike now understood. When everyone was seated, David's case was called. David and Mike stood up, and the charges were read.

The judge asked David if he understood the charges. David replied, "Good morning your honor, yes. I understand the charges as read."

The judge asked Mike, "How does your client plead?"

Mike replied, "Good morning your honor. My client pleads not guilty, and we are asking a reasonable bail to be set since my client has no criminal record and is not a flight risk. My client is prepared to post bail."

The judge asked the new prosecutor, "Does the government have any objections to bail being granted?"

The new prosecutor stated, "No your honor." There was silence for a moment.

Mike leaned over to David as said, "Maybe Ray talked him into it."

David replied, "No. This is not the doing of the new prosecutor. This judge is on Vincent's payroll. Watch, he's going to deny bail."

After a moment, the judge spoke up. "Bail is at the discretion of the court. Due to the sensitive nature of this case and those involved, bail is denied. The defendant will be remanded to the custody of the Federal Marshall's. Is the government ready to proceed with scheduling a pre-trial date?"

The prosecutor responded, "We are still gathering some last minute evidence your honor."

"How much time do you need? Are you aware of the caseload facing this court?"

"I am your honor. We should only need two more weeks."

The judge replied, "Fine. The preliminary trial is set for three weeks from today."

Mike asked, "Your honor, we have never been given the real identity of the victim in this tragic event. Can that be provided to us? It is my client's right for his legal staff to have all pertinent information, so we can adequately prepare?"

The judge responded, "The court orders that the identification of the victim is disclosed to the defense. The court further orders that the identity of the victim is not to be disclosed in any form and must remain confidential. Follow the rules of discovery counselor."

Mike replied, "Thank you, your honor. I only ask that the court reconsiders its decision to deny bail."

The judge replied, "You have my ruling counselor. If you wish to file an appeal, you know the process."

Mike replied, "Thank you, your honor."

David was taken into custody, and Mike spoke to Ray and the new prosecutor in a private room. Mike was furious and asked, "What the hell just happened in here?"

The new prosecutor said, "How the hell do I know. I did not object to bail. Ray filled me in on everything. I didn't even know a new judge was picked."

Mike replied, "David was right. This judge is probably as crooked as the path to Oz. What else could it be?" Sarcastically Mike asked, "So new guy, how are we going to play this?"

The prosecutor said, "First, there's no need for that. My name is John. As for how we are going to play this; I am going to do my job, and you are going to do yours. If we are both smart, we will get to the truth. If we are going to be idiots, and this judge is crooked, your client will go away for a long time. Does that sum it up for you?"

Mike replied, "I'm sorry John. What I said was not necessary. Please understand with the relationship my client has had with Ray and the bureau, this was the last thing we expected."

John said, "Forget it, I understand. Ray's word and reputation are like gold to me. Now let's find out the truth."

Mike said, "I'll send the paperwork for discovery to your office today."

John said, "Yes, please do that. Let's make it official. However, off the record, Max's real name is Sheldon Philips."

Mike said, "Thank you. Can I have a few minutes with my client?"

John said, "He's already waiting for you in room A."

Everyone shook hands and went their own way.

It was well after eleven. They expected to hear from David by now. As it approached eleven-thirty, they really started to worry. Lou knew he could not call. Maybe another case was called first. So many things could have happened. He called Charlie, who was waiting outside the courtroom for David. Charlie told Mike asked him not to call until he had all the details, and he would call Lou. At the same time, Mike was calling through. Lou told him he would call him back. Mike had to get all the information where David would be held before he called. Lou told Mike he was with the girls and putting his call on speaker. It took Mike a minute to gather his thoughts. He told them everything. Exactly how it happened.

Lou was furious and asked, "How is David?"

Mike replied, "Lou. He knew it already. He wasn't shocked."

Lou thanked him for all he tried to do and explained he knew it was not his fault.

Lou added, "I'm going to call Russell now. We have to step this up."

"Don't bother. Russell knows. He was waiting outside the courtroom. I guess David called him on his way to the bureau yesterday. David knew this was going to happen. He called it in the courtroom."

Lou said, "Okay, what's a good time to set up a call with you and Russ?"

Mike replied, "Let's make it six o'clock tonight."

Molly was in shock, and Allie was crying. All she could say was, "I knew it. I just knew it. I felt it yesterday when he left. I knew he wasn't coming home."

Lou could not afford to get emotional. He also knew he had to keep the girls stay focused. He could not do everything that needed to be done and keep the girls on track at the same time. He had to stay focused. In Allie's case and David's appeals, he had David to help him. Lou was not a criminal lawyer. He would not have David here to help. He learned a great deal from David, but not enough. He knew he had to rely on Mike, Russell, and maybe even Paulie. Lou explained all of this to the girls. They were strong. They only needed to get out some emotions. They reassured Lou that he could count on them to be strong so he could focus on helping David. At one-thirty Russell called. Lou and Russell exchanged information. Paulie had arrived at the house as soon as he heard. Paulie knew he would have to be there for Lou. This was not just another case; this was Lou's son. He was not going to lose him to some crooked judge and crime boss. Lou was prepared for battle, and it was going to be a big one. After venting, everyone calmed down. About three o'clock Lou's phone rang again. It was not a number in his contacts since this was his private phone. He was still with Molly, Allie, and Paulie. When Maria heard of this from Paulie, she left work early. She stopped by the store and came to the house to make dinner so the girls would not have to. Molly and Allie appreciated that but insisted on helping. They needed to stay busy. By this time, Maria was like family. She was more than Paulie's fiancé.

The call was from David. Both Ray and John had it set up that David could make outgoing calls whenever he needed to. He was not being held in a maximum-security facility. He was at the Federal Marshall's building which had a few holding cells. Ray and John pulled some strings. David was not being held in a typical jail or prison facility. Everyone was happy to hear from David. He explained he was fine, and would probably be there for a while. He told them he would call every day.

Allie asked, "When can I visit you?"

"I don't want you here just yet. Russell is working on some things right now. He will explain when you talk at six. He is going to tell you things. You all have to listen and follow his instructions. Remember, these calls are taped. I have no idea who listens to them. Anything important you need to tell me can go through him, Mike, or Paulie. Russell only lives thirty minutes from here. Dad, you, Mike, Russell, and Paulie are on the do not tape call list because you are part of my legal team. Even with that, I would be careful. Ray will explain."

Paulie said, "Dave, you hang in there. I have spoken with Russ and will fill them in before everyone talks later."

David said, "Thanks. Mom, don't worry. Everything will be fine. Let me talk to Allie."

Allie and David spoke for about ten minutes. Most of the time it was regarding the baby, and how much they missed each other. After a few minutes, David told her he would call tomorrow.

Everyone sat down for dinner and ate. With all this going on, Lou was surprised everyone was in decent spirits. He knew this was going to be a rough road. Lou was hoping to hear good news from Russ. At least Paulie coming on board was going well. Russ said he was a natural. Clark, his parole officer, was not having any issues with him. Paulie was on the right track to turn his life around. Paulie and Maria announced they had set a date for their wedding. It would be next spring in May. It was just about six when Lou's phone rang. Everyone was sitting around the table when Lou answered it. It was Russell. Everyone exchanged greetings. Lou started it off.

"Russ, what do you have for us?"

"Before we get started, I need to say one thing. It is imperative that everyone does exactly as I say. David's future is going to depend on each step that everyone takes. I have to know I can count on each of you." Everyone agreed.

Russ went on to say, "I know today was a shock to everyone, but it wasn't to David. Something like this was exactly what he expected, and we have been preparing for it."

Lou asked, "Why the hell didn't anyone let us in on this?"

Russ replied, "Lou, sometimes the fewer people that know things, the better. David and I had to see how things played out and see if David's hunch was right. If everyone knew and treated Ray differently, he would know. We would lose our advantage. Let me recap what we know at this point t. This will go to pre-trial. If we do not come up with something in the next two to three weeks, they have enough for it to go to trial. Accept that. If what we believe is true, and if we can find the evidence we need, we do not want to have David cleared of this before it goes to trial. If that happens, the ones behind this will not get the justice they deserve. Mind you, this is only our theory. We may be wrong, and none of this will pan out. If that happens, then there is a real possibility David can get convicted."

Allie started to speak, and Russ interrupted saying, "Allie. I know what everyone wants to say. Please don't, and just listen. You can ask me anything you want after."

You could hear a pin drop in the room it was so quiet.

Russ went on to say, "David thinks the man that approached him murdered Max. He also thinks he stole the knife from his s trunk while it was parked in the garage at the hotel overnight. David believes the girl is a setup to help frame him. At first, he suspected Ray but changed his mind after he saw all that Ray did to get him held where he is. I do not totally trust John, the new prosecutor, at least not yet. I believe as David does that the judge is on Vincent's payroll. This is all a great theory and makes sense, but we need to prove it. Only Ray is aware of this. He is checking out John, but even with that, we're not ready to let him in on this yet."

Lou asked, "It's a good theory and makes perfect sense. How can we prove it?'

Russ said, "Paulie, why don't you take it from here?"

Paulie said, "We have put some things in motion. First, I went back to David's hotel. There were more surveillance videos in the manager's office. However, David's car was blocked by a large structural support that was located by the space where his car was parked. We do not have a full visual on the entire car. We do have an unidentified man on the tape that appeared to be walking towards David's car, but he is not seen when he walks past the support. He was wearing a sweatshirt with the hood up. We cannot identify him. The footage is not very clear. It is difficult to get height, weight, and those types of things. However, it's good enough to get a rough idea if we had something to compare it against. Keep in mind, it does not show him going into the trunk because the valet attendant backed David's car into the parking space. We do not have that view. We are still checking all the other cameras to see if he shows up somewhere else inside or outside of the garage. Hopefully, we will get the make and model of the car he was in or a plate number."

Paulie went on to say, "We sent a team to the garage. The attendant saved the ticket. They save those in the event the customer needs it later as a receipt. He showed us where David's car was parked. Although it's been some time, we received permission from the hotel manager to take samples of the flooring. We took it all sides of the car. If Ray cooperates, we can get a warrant for the clothing and shoes of the man who approached David. That might tie him to the garage; however, he can claim that is a coincidence since we have nothing that shows him doing anything to David's car. We also went back to where Max was found and extended the area to outside the building to search for any evidence such as footprints, tire marks, and things like that. However, there was a fire there and many firefighters. Between all the firefighters and fire apparatus, we don't expect that will turn anything up, but we don't want to miss any opportunities."

Paulie went on to say, "As for the female witness, we are running her. We found some inconsistencies that we are looking into. Lastly, I called in some favors. I gave her picture to a couple of people when I was in the city to see if they recognized her. They did not, but they were going to check around. Maybe we can tie her into that crowd somehow. The other person we are checking out is the federal judge. If he is dirty, he might be in someone's book. I reached out to a few more people. I wasn't that high up in the ranks but did many favors for people. They owe me, and things are so messed up now; no one knows who is doing what. If we are going to find anything out, it has to be now before things tighten up. Trust me, they will. I know not all of this sounds promising. There are many what ifs. However, it only takes is one thing to pan out. Maybe we can get someone to talk. We have to try every angle."

Lou asked, "Can I make a suggestion?"

"Of course," Russell replied.

"Does it make sense to canvas the area? There is an apartment building right across the street from the garage. Should we canvas that building? People take pictures of everything on their cell phones nowadays. Maybe someone saw something and didn't report it because they didn't want to get involved."

Russell replied, "Excellent idea. I will get someone on it."

Allie added, "You know there's a coffee shop across from the entrance to the garage. It might take a bit, but people who are regular coffee goers might remember seeing something, or seeing that man there."

Paulie responded, "I'll work on that Russ."

Lou said, "At least we are off to a start. Maybe your team will find something on David's car that will help. Has anything come back on Max's clothes?"

Russ replied, "Actually yes. They identified some chemicals or something on his clothes that might tell them where he was before he was moved to that building. The lab is analyzing the particulates. This could be a break. I am sure they expected most of the evidence to be burned in the fire. If we can determine where Max was killed, that will be a home run."

Lou asked, "Does David know all of this?

Russ replied, "David knows everything."

Lou also asked, "And Ray?"

Russ said, "Well, this is what we need to discuss. How much are we going to trust Ray?"

Lou replied, "Honestly, in my opinion, completely. If Ray were a part of this, things would be going much different, and now that David is in custody, he would have stopped you from gaining access to anything until the FBI was done. He is letting us work side-by-side."

"I agree. What does everyone else think?" Everyone agreed. It was decided. Russ would keep Ray in the loop on everything unless something came up that would be a reason to stop. Russ said, "Don't worry Lou. I will coordinate with Mike and Ray regarding everything. I will filter things down through Paulie since he is working so closely on this. I will be swamped working on this. Paulie will keep you all up-to-speed. I think your main focus should be on your family." Everyone agreed.

CHAPTER 9

WHEN THINGS GET STICKY

Many times, things do not go as smooth as we would like. These issues being checked were shots in the dark. However, the girls were optimistic. Lou did not want to discourage them. He knew things would begin to get sticky. His biggest concern was trust. Could they trust Ray, or for some reason, did he lose his loyalty? Lou knew Ray had high aspirations for a promotion, and could not help but wonder if David would be a pawn in this game. The next few days would tell a big story.

*****

Over the next few days, they had not heard much. Paulie was away for three days and spoke to Lou each day to keep him informed. Checking the outside of the building where Max was found turned-up nothing. The scene was too disrupted by the fire, apparatus, and personnel. Anything they recovered held no value to the case or their theory. They might have caught a break with the traffic cam videos. There was a shot of a car that had the man who approached David driving it. It was only one block from the parking garage. That alone was not enough evidence because it does not place him in the garage and by David's car. They took samples of everything every place they checked for analysis. Ray's team took additional samples of materials found at the scene of the fire. They also went back to the hotel parking lot and took additional samples of all the materials found on the ground, the support, the railing at the rear of the car, and out twenty feet out.

They also went to the hotel Max was staying at and took carpet samples in his room, the hallways, and stairwells. They hoped that some particulates might match up and tie different places together. All of their findings were given to Ray. Russell was waiting to see if they could get a warrant for the man who approached David, Joseph Rivera. He wanted to check his clothes and shoes. Any hope of finding any matching forensic evidence was being looked at. They had to prove and place him in the hotel-parking garage by David's car.

Russell was keeping David informed of everything. Many of these ideas were his. David spoke to his family daily. The last time he spoke with his dad, Lou wanted to let him know of his trust issues.

David replied, "Dad. I have full trust in Ray. Talk to Paulie, he can explain more. I can't say much on this line since this call is logged as a personal call, not an attorney call. Everything we discuss should be in person, rather than by phone."

Lou replied, "I understand. Do not worry. Take care of yourself."

Lou felt very uncomfortable that he did not know everything. He wasn't used to this. He was always in the loop. Lou did not call Paulie. He called Russell to find out what David was referring to and wanted to express his concerns. A little over a week had passed since David was taken into custody. It seemed they were no further along. Russell did not answer his phone. Lou left a voice message. Russ sent him a text informing him he was with David, and then had to check on some additional things. He would call him first thing in the morning. The following day Russell called Lou. The first thing Lou discussed was his concerns about not knowing everything as it happened.

"Lou, I understand your frustration, but it has to be this way. Please try to understand, many things are going on. I do not want people calling each other and clouding any issues. It is easier to funnel information this way. I cannot forget how your family was almost destroyed during Allie's case. I do not want to see that happen again. I really want you to focus on Molly, Allie, and the baby."

Lou replied, "You're right. It's not easy. So what's going on?"

"We have a lot that we are working on. We hit some roadblocks. You know we got nothing from the outside of building Max was found in, and the traffic cam videos are not much help without more supporting evidence. Unfortunately, the coffee shop across the street has no video from that day. I could not call you back last night because I received additional information I needed to evaluate before I called. They found out where Max was murdered."

Lou asked, "Where?"

"He was murdered in a stairwell of the hotel garage where David was staying. There were no cameras in the hallway. Another camera picked up a white van that was parked by the entrance to the stairway door. The side door of the Van was facing the stairwell opening. The van blocked the camera from seeing that side of the van, or the door. We have the license plate number. It turns out the van was rented that day by David, or should I say someone posing as David. I spoke to the car rental people last night. The rental was made by phone, and payment was made by a fake credit card account. Their fax shows that they received an electronic signature and copy of David's license via fax. We are tracing back where the fax came from, but we expect it will be from some type of faxing service and not a reliable address. The van was picked up the night before after closing. Therefore, the keys were left in a secure pickup box. I have already dusted the box for prints. None of the prints matched anyone on file. They were probably wearing gloves. The FBI has the van and traces of the same plastic that Max was wrapped in that were found in the back of the van. Furthermore, during the autopsy, there were particulates from the garage on Max's clothing. I am convinced this is a frame. If it were a hit, Max's body would have never been found. Whoever did this, knew this evidence would be found. If David had done this, he would know enough not to leave this type of trial."

Lou said, "They almost have a rock-solid case against him."

Russell replied, "Yes. They do. However, it's not over." The other roadblocks we hit were very interesting. It took three days to get the warrant for Rivera's clothing and shoes. Ray had the judge who handled Allie's case sign the warrants to seize them. This is also interesting. As you are aware, the judge handling the case usually signs the warrants. Because Paulie had not heard from his contacts, Ray did not want to run the risk that this judge would deny the warrants. Within an hour of the warrants being executed, the new judge called the judge who signed the warrants and blasted him for doing it. He claimed he did not have the authority to sign them since he would have denied them. By the way, our friend handled it quite well. It does give me a higher degree of suspicion that this judge is corrupt. We are less than two weeks from the preliminary trial and running out of time. I have every available man working on this."

Lou replied, "Thanks for everything, but it looks like we're going to need a miracle. They really did a good job of planning this."

Russell replied, "Don't worry. I figure it all out. There has to be a trail somewhere. We are still canvassing the hotel across the street from the garage and the coffee shop. We should have that completed in the next couple of days. I have someone in the coffee shop every day talking to the customers. Something might break. Don't lose hope."

Lou replied, "Never. I want you to know I am not planning to tell the girls this news. Please ask Paulie not to tell them anything. I want them to think all is going well. I know something will turn up." Things are getting sticky.

Russell replied, "I understand. We will talk soon. We don't have everything back on David's car yet." Lou felt helpless. He knew if anyone could break this tangled web, Russell could. Paulie stopped in the office shortly after the call. He could see how upset Lou was and knew he must have spoken with Russell. When Paulie sat down, he said, "Lou, please don't worry. We'll figure this out." Lou said I know Paulie. This is only a preliminary trial to see if there is enough evidence for it to go to a jury trial. I was hoping that this would be done by then, and the charges dropped so David could come home." Paulie replied, "Something will break. I still haven't heard from my contacts yet." It was lunchtime. Allie and Molly walked in to take Lou to lunch. Since Paulie was there, they called

Maria, and everyone met at the Café for lunch. They did not talk about the case at all. When they first asked, Lou said things were going well, and they were starting to put everything together.

Meanwhile, business was going well for Molly and Allie. After the reviews were published, the Allie M. line took off and went global. Orders were piling up. The girls were going to interview people for two additional associate positions that were desperately needed. Allie, Molly, and their staff were doing the best they could; however, between David's situation, and business, it was hard to be focused. They were both working long hours. Allie did not want to be away from the baby this much. They were already working on the spring line as well. The building they rented was very large. It had plenty of room for growth, now, needed to hire additional people. They contacted the agency they used in New York the last time to help find another experienced person and would try to hire locally for just the routine day-to-day things. In one way, this was a blessing. It helped to keep the girls focused. However, deep inside; Allie was holding so much back. She cried herself to sleep every night. The last time Allie was pregnant, she knew it before she missed her next menstrual cycle, or any morning sickness started. She was having that same feeling and did not want to tell anyone. She made an appointment to see the doctor. She was pregnant. This made her very happy, but also sad, because David wasn't there to share in the news. She was wondering if should she tell him now, or wait. The pre-trial was next week. Since she and Molly thought things were going well, David would probably be home soon. She decided to wait to tell everyone when David returned. What a great welcome home present that would make.

As luck would have it, the agency called within two days and had a perfect candidate for them. They set up an interview for the end of the week. One of the young mother's in town had stopped working when her second son was born and applied for the other position. Now that her son was old enough to be in daycare, she wanted to get back to work. She had excellent office skills since she worked as a personal secretary and assistant. She was a perfect fit. They hired her on the spot. Allie and Molly already knew her. They were not aware she was looking to go back to work. She heard through the grapevine that Allie and Molly were looking for someone and went right over. It was a good match. Her name was June. June would handle all their personal affairs such as appointments, and run the office. This would free up a tremendous amount of their time. The design layout and order processing people were very happy since they were starting to feel a bit overwhelmed having to handle some of these other things as well as doing their job. Business was good. They could afford it. Allie and Molly needed to spend their time designing. At some point, they would need to start traveling from time to time to other shows. Magazines and articles are not enough in this business to keep up with the trend, although, Allie wanted to be more of the trendsetter. They also knew at some point, they might have to scale up their line a bit. The trend at the time was the loose and blousy appearance. However, there was still a huge market for those women who wanted a slimmer fitting garment. They were afraid of growing too fast before they were completely established.

*****

The end of the week arrived, and they had the interview with the person the agency recommended. She was young, single, and loved the fashion industry. She was well known within the industry since she used to be a model. She had gotten tired of trying to keep up with all the younger girls coming into the business, but knew the industry inside and out. She was the perfect candidate for the account specialist position they wanted to fill. The person in this position could work from a home office in the event they did not want to relocate. Besides working from her office, it also involved some traveling, which was a perfect mix for this individual. She lived just outside the city limits of New York, which is where she would have to most of the time. The interview went great. She was a great fit, and they hired her. They would give her a computer that networked into their system. She would have access to everything she needed, and they could have video conference calls. This computer was for work only and fully encrypted for security reasons. Allie missed David so much. As much as everyone was like family, she always felt like the third wheel. Whenever they went out to dinner, or people were at the house, it was always, Lou, Molly, Paulie, Maria, and Allie. All her life Allie was a loner. She finally had a husband, a life, and a family she always wanted. She had gotten used to it. That night they all met for dinner at "The Café." All the girls could feel how stressed Lou and Paulie were. The pre-trial was starting soon. If all was going well, why did they appear so stressed? Finally, Molly could not stand it anymore.

She said, "David is my son too. If things were going well, you would not seem so stressed. I have never seen you this way. Don't let us be shocked next week. If there is something we need to know, tell us now."

Lou looked up at Paulie and was silent for a moment. Paulie gave him a nod, his way of saying; tell them. Lou said, "Okay, we are stressed. It's simple. Unless some new findings coming out or something breaks, they have more than enough evidence to hold David over for trial. We are not giving up. It's only round one, but there is a chance he won't be coming home next week."

Allie said, "I'm pregnant."

Molly replied, "Did I just hear you right? You're pregnant?"

Allie said, "Yes. I'm pregnant." As the last word came from her mouth, both Allie, Molly, and Maria started to cry.

Were these happy or sad tears, or maybe a combination of both? Allie could not keep it a secret anymore, especially now facing the reality that David may not come home next week. David had been speaking to everyone every day. He never led on how the case was progressing. He always sounded so confident. Allie asked, "Should I tell David? I thought he would be home next week and the news would make coming home even more special for him." Everyone was emotionally drained.

Paulie broke the silence and said, "Tell him."

Allie asked, "Do you think I should? Does he need that additional stress right now?"

Paulie said, "David knows exactly what is going on. He has accepted the fact that he will probably be held over for trial. Some of what we are trying to find out will take time. Three weeks is not enough time. He needs something else to give him hope. Remember, we all have each other. He is sitting there alone."

Everyone agreed that David should be told. Their tears were now happy ones. When David called that night, Allie would tell him. They had a nice dinner and decided not to have coffee there. Molly suggested they all come back to the house. David would be calling at eight. He needs to now we all know the situation and are supporting him. Allie can tell him then.

When they got to the house, Paulie explained that when they speak by phone, they talk in code, meaning, they refer to things by number. Number one meant canvasing the apartment, number two meant, canvassing the coffee shop. On Monday, the forensic reports would be back on Rivera's shoes and clothing. If they were positive for a match to the scrapings from the garage, that would be good, but still not be enough. They needed to find some evidence in David's car. Paulie further explained that his friend Johnny was still passing the photo around of the witness the FBI claims to have and checking to see if the new judge was tied to Vincent in any way. He explained this would be a slow process. If he were suspected of anything, that could get him killed. Everybody in the organization is watching each other. No one knows whom to trust. Rivera was running things, or he was the front person for Vincent.

Paulie said, "I sure all the orders still come from Vincent. The only good thing is Rivera is stupid. He is not as smart as Vincent is. He is too visible. He wants to have his hands in everything. No one ever saw Vincent. Something has to break."

Lou said, "I hope so. I hate to see David serve ten years like Allie did before we're able to get these answers."

Paulie replied, "There is one more person I am going to reach out to. Ray, Russell, and I have been talking about what kind of deal we can make so he will roll over. The problem is, we do not have enough on him to use that as a bargaining chip, but he is now Rivera's right-hand man. I did a lot for him. Business was really suffering within the family. No one would do business with them until all of this passed. Rivera put the word out that he was looking for a source. Maybe we'll get lucky."

Lou replied, "At this point, all we have left is luck."

About five minutes later the phone rang. It was David. Lou answered and told David he was on speakerphone. He told David not to be mad, but everyone sensed the stress and knew everything. This was a recorded call. Everyone needed to be careful what he or she said.

David replied, "Don't worry. I figured it would come to that eventually. It's probably better this way."

David asked if Paulie was there. Lou told him everyone was on the line.

David asked, "Paulie, did you ever find those two items that I asked you to look for?"

"I've been looking for both items. I have not found either of them yet. I'll have a chance to go through the bins again over the weekend."

David said, "Thanks."

Molly told him all that was going on and the new people they hired. David thought that was great and was very proud of them. They never gave up. People should never give up. Something always changes. They understood what he meant.

Allie said, "Babe, I have something to tell you."

David laughed and replied, "Well I couldn't have done anything wrong. Tell me."

Allie said, "I'm pregnant."

David yelled out, "AWESOME! When did you find out?"

"Remember when I got pregnant with Louis? I just felt it. Well, I had that same feeling and went to the doctors a few days ago. She ran the test and told me."

"I won't get mad you didn't tell me sooner. I understand. However, in the future promise me there will be no more holding things back. I can handle it.

Allie replied, "Alright. I promise. Are you excited?"

"Really, you are going to ask me that? Of course I am."

Allie asked, "What are you hoping for, a boy, or a girl?"

"A healthy baby is what I want. If I had to choose, you know what that is. We have talked about it. I would like a girl."

Allie replied, "Me too."

David laughed and said, "We have another thing in common."

Allie asked, "What's that babe?"

"When you got pregnant with Louis, we found out while you were in jail. This time you found out you are pregnant while I am in jail. If you get pregnant again, I hope that doesn't mean we're both be in jail?"

Allie replied, "You're an idiot, but I love you."

David replied, "Love you too. I have to go now. See you soon."

David's time on the call was up and had to hang up. He told everyone not to worry. Everything would work out. After the call, everyone seemed more relaxed. David sounded hopeful, joking, and happy to hear the news. They both wanted a girl. They wanted Molly to have a granddaughter. They already chose a name. If it was a girl, they wanted to name her Jessica, after David's sister who was killed when she was eight years old. They would not tell Molly until after the baby was born. A secret they vowed to keep. They were hoping for a girl. They knew how happy Molly would be. Everyone enjoyed the moment then decided to call it a night. Paulie would have a busy weekend, and the following week was going to be stressful. After Paulie and Maria left, Molly said, "Give the baby to Lou. Sit with me and let me hold you." Allie and Molly sat on the couch. Molly held Allie while Lou played with the baby. David let the baby hear his voice every time he called. That was very hard, yet important to him.

After a while, everyone got up. Allie had to put the baby to bed and wanted to get some sleep. She would find it easier to sleep tonight.

Over the weekend, Russell and Paulie did nothing but put a large push on talking to everyone they had missed in the apartment building and the coffee shop. After two days, they came up with nothing. Sunday night when Lou, Russell, Mike, and Paulie spoke, they all knew they had nothing concrete that would save this from going to trial. You cannot rush forensic science. It is a painstaking process. Missing the slightest thing could mean the difference in winning or losing a case. Russell got back the results on Rivera's clothes. Both his shoes and pants had the exact same particulates on them as those from around David's car. In itself, this could only introduce doubt, but alone, would not get David off. The results from the White Van would not come back before the pre-trial, and although the FBI team was done with David's car, Russell's team was still working on it. Those results would also not be back in time. To make a strong argument, they would have to be able to tie Rivera to the parking garage, the van, and David's car. This along with their findings on Max's clothes, would place Rivera at the murder scene, and every place that Max's body was. That would no longer be considered reasonable doubt because there would now be actual evidence. If it came together, it would not be in time for the pre-trial on Tuesday, and probably not enough to get the charges dropped.

When they were speaking, Russell said, "Everyone makes a mistake. They miss something. Vincent's first mistake was making this personal by trying to frame David, rather than just getting rid of Max's body. All we have to do is find out what they missed. Mike, how do you think Tuesday will go?"

Mike replied, "The FBI brass wants this wrapped up. Depending on the judge, which is still questionable, I think it is going to trial. Jury selection will start the following week, and the main trial will start the week after if a jury is selected."

Russ asked, "Can you stall that?"

Mike said, "I doubt it. There is tremendous pressure from above on this, and they have enough evidence for a conviction. It may not be up to the prosecuting attorney. He will have to do what he is told. Gentleman, we've been granted a lot of freedom here."

At that moment, Paulie's phone rang. It was his connection, Johnny. He told Paulie someone recognized the girl in the picture from one of the parties and was trying to get a name. He also told Paulie he heard that Rivera found a source to get some product. He was still working on that, but it would take some time.

Johnny added, "I can't afford to arouse suspicion. Rivera is an idiot. He is involved with everything. This went right to his head." Paulie told him to stay in contact and be careful, and not to do anything stupid.

Paulie told everyone, "Johnny will not be able to get all the information we need without people wondering why he's asking around. Johnny was not involved as long as I was. I have to go back to the city and get to my other contact."

Russ asked, "Who is that?"

Paulie replied, "I can't say right now. I'll check into it when I go to the city in the morning."

Russ said, "Wait. Lou, can you get Ray on this call?

Lou said, "I'll try." He called Ray, and Ray answered. They filled him in on all of this information.

Ray said, "God, this is going to be a mess. I cannot act on any of this without proof. Do you realize what you're doing?"

Paulie said, "I can handle this. I have one question though. I do not want to put the cart before the horse. The one thing I know is the players involved. I know what and how they will do things. Ray, are you prepared to offer up to three deals?"

"I can't make those promises Paulie. It depends on what we're getting in return."

Paulie said, "Fair enough. As long as I know the possibility is on the table."

Ray replied, "The possibility is always on the table. Let's see where this goes."

Paulie suggested, "If I get what I think I could get, just be ready at a moment's notice if I call."

Ray said, "You got it."

They were running out of time. The preliminary trial was only three days away. They did not have enough to get the charges dropped. David would be held over for trial. Russell's people were working frantically on David's car. They even went back to the parking garage. So far, nothing has turned up. It would take not one, but a series of miracles to keep David out of jail, or worse. Murdering a federal agent carries the death penalty. No one wanted to think of that possibility. Either way, David could get a life sentence. No one, especially Maria, liked the fact that Pauline was going into the city to dig deeper. No one knew where and whom he would be talking with. Russell was going to have two people follow him, but he knew they could only go so far. If anything went wrong, they might not be able to protect him. This was something Paulie had to do. He owned everything he had today to David. He had to be there for him at any cost.

Paulie was up and gone before anyone got up. While driving into the city, he went over all the possibilities in his mind. He knew some things for sure. The witness they had was definitely tied to the organization because some recognized her picture. Johnny was just a captain with his own territory like Paulie. He did not have the upscale connections. He would need him to get to his other connection to talk. Paulie could not risk contacting him directly, and they had to meet privately. He knew the organization was not doing business, and money had to be a problem. Rivera was stupid. He didn't think. He just reacted, which was why he was trying to make another connection for drugs. The other families involved had their own problems and the families not involved, would not touch them for fear of exposing their operations. Rivera always like this person, they called Junior. He made Junior his right-hand man. If anyone knew anything, Junior did. Junior was his connection. Early in the days when Paulie was involved with the family, Junior was trying to make a name for himself. He tried setting up a deal. Junior was originally an enforcer, a leg breaker. He performed some contract killings and had a long arrest record, including some prison time. This was his life. It was all he knew. Paulie remembered finding out that the deal was going down in his territory. He found out the details and showed up with some men when the deal was going down. Junior, as stupid as he was, went alone. Trying to make the big score to impress Vincent and maybe get a territory of his own.

The deal went bad, and the people he was dealing with were going to rip him off. When Paulie and his crew showed up, they were giving Junior a beaten. They would have killed him for sure. Paulie and his crew saved his life. Paulie did not want a war. He only wanted to protect Junior. His crew gave these dealers one hell of a beating, let them keep their product, and told them never to come back. He knew if he kept their product that would start a war. Junior owed Paulie his life. It was time to collect. Paulie arrived in the city around ten a.m. He got a room in a dumpy hotel where they did not know him and called Johnny. This was a hotel where no one had eyes are ears. They minded their own business. Paulie could not afford to be seen. By now, the word got around what he was doing for a living. No one would trust him. He had to play Junior. Make him think he knew more than he did to get the information he needed. He liked Junior and wanted to try to get him to turn. This would be a cat and mouse game. Paulie chose this hotel because years back, he and Junior took a couple of women there. They laughed about it. The room number they were in was room number 69. They joked about it so many times; he knew Junior would never forget, or at least he hoped he had not. When he called Johnny, he said, I don't want you to get in any deeper. Call Junior. Tell him to meet me in our room. He'll understand. Tell him to come alone, and be here at one o'clock. Tell him he owes me that. He'll know what you mean.

Paulie told Johnny to call him back when he got the message to Junior. He said, "Johnny, use your head. Forget you ever got this call and stay out of this. I appreciated all you have found out for me. But now, your life depends on you listening to me."

After about ten minutes, Johnny called Paulie back and told him Junior got the message and would be there.

"Johnny, remember. Forget this now and move on. Don't be stupid."

Johnny replied, "I don't want to know anything. Things are too hot right now."

Paulie was tough, but also a bit scared. No one knew where he was. If anything happened, no one would receive whatever information he might receive. He decided he had to trust someone. He called Russell. When Russell picked up the phone, he explained his plan. Russell told him he knew where he was. He just didn't know the room number until Paulie just told him. Russell told him he had a couple of his people tail him as a precaution.

Russell asked, "Why the hell didn't you tell me. I could have wired the room before you got there."

Paulie said, "I had no idea the room would be available. I know Junior will check me. I couldn't wear a wire."

Russell replied, "Forget it, its history. My people are outside in a white van with a plumbing company's advertisement on it. I'll call you when Junior arrives. He's in the database. I have his picture. I'll let you know if he's alone. If he's not, get the hell out of there and get to the van. Open a window by the street, and try to talk near it. Maybe my people could pick something up with our microphones. It won't look funny if you are looking out the window like you are watching the street. Paulie agreed.

Paulie had picked up a sub and sat down to eat. It was about eleven-thirty. He had some time to kill. As he kept going over his plan in his head, the time was getting closer. He was feeling more anxious. At ten minutes to one, Russell called to let Paulie know that Junior arrived and was alone. He was on his way up. It was show time. What Paulie didn't know, was Russell also called Ray. Ray had four agents in two cars parked about one block away in case things went bad. Pauline heard a knock on the door. It was Junior. Paulie opened the door, and Junior walked in. They exchanged a hug. They were quite close at one time.

Junior said to Paulie, "Hey. You know I have to check."

Paulie replied, "I understand."

Junior patted him down and found no weapons or wires. Paulie did the same. They both sat down. Junior asked, "So what's this all about?"

Paulie said, "Junior. No one but you and Johnny knows I'm here. I can't take that risk. Let me give it to you straight. Everyone knows no product is coming in. The police are arresting every hooker who walks the streets. No games are around, and the other families won't touch you. The word on the street is, Rivera found a new source and is bringing in product. If I heard it, you know damn well the Feds did as well. What are you thinking? This fool is an idiot. Vincent never was directly involved. We knew where the orders came from, but we never got them directly from Vincent. Rivera is like a walking time bomb. He will take you down with him."

Junior replied, "What the hell am I supposed to do. I'm his right-hand man. I can't let him go it alone."

"Junior, give me the details. I will let the Feds know where I got the info. They will also arrest you, and you will disappear in the program."

Junior said. "I'm not a rat!"

"Look at it this way. You and I both know the Feds will find out whether you tell me or not. You will catch a pinch. With your record, you will go away for life with the amount of product I hear is coming in. As for Rivera, eventually, he will roll and protect himself."

Junior replied, "You're right about one thing. Rivera will save his own ass."

"Well, you're a fool if you don't protect yourself. Rivera knows a lot of shit. He will make a deal. The organization is falling apart. You know that as well as I do. When this shit blows over, the other families will send their people, split the territory, and run it. You'll either be left out in the cold or killed."

Junior sat back for a few minutes and thought about all of this. He said, "Your right. If I stay in, I can't win. I guess I have to do this.

I have to tell you something. I owe you my life, and here you are trying to protect me again."

During this time, Paulie walked over to the window many times to try to help Russell get this on tape, Junior sitting close to the window. With any luck, Russell got it all on tape.

Junior said, "The product is coming in a week from today at the docks. There will only be one boat at the pier. They will be meeting at one o'clock in the morning. I also know things about your friend David. I'll have to tell you later. I have to meet the boss at two-thirty. If I'm late, he'll be suspicious. Paulie, I trust you."

"I never let you down, and I won't now. You have to tell me about David. He saved my life. I owe him."

Junior said, "I can't right now. You'll know it all soon enough."

Paulie didn't want to push him and said, "Okay, get out of here. We'll be seeing each other soon."

When Junior left, he called Russell and Ray. Ray called them back on a secure line. Paulie gave him the heads-up on the product coming in. Ray told them he would take care of that and get the whole bunch. Paulie asked, "Ray, you have to get Junior in the program."

Ray replied, "If this goes down, we'll make it look good, and he'll be in. He has to give it all up."

"He will. He has never gone back on his word to me. He also knows something about David but did not have time to tell me. He had to leave to meet Rivera. I didn't want to push him. That would make him suspicious, and I didn't want him to back out."

Ray said, "Good call. We'll find out soon enough. If this does not go down, we will pick him up and squeeze him until we get that information. Sorry Paulie, once we pick him up and release him, he'll get whacked. Rivera won't know whether he talked or not and won't take that chance. One way or another, we will get what we need. We can leverage him and tell him we are putting the word out on the streets that he talked. He'll have no choice but to cooperate."

Russell said, "Either way it goes, it sounds like a good plan."

"I'm leaving now. I can't be seen in the city. I'm heading back."

Russell and Ray said, "We'll have our people follow you out of town."

Paulie started to head out of town. He saw Russell's van a few cars back. He assumed the agents were around as well. Shortly after he got on Parkway heading out of the city, a van came up fast on his left. The side door opened, and shots rang out. Paulie was hit. His car ran up against the side of a bridge abutment. Russell's van stopped. There was one agent's car in front of Paulie, and one behind Russ's van. When the agents in the rear saw the other van coming up fast, they passed Russ's van. As soon as the shots were fired, the car in front blocked the road. They had the shooters blocked in. They called for an ambulance. Paulie was alive, but bleeding badly. He was shot just under his left arm. If he hadn't ducked, he would probably be dead. As the ambulance was taking him away, and just before he passed out, he told Russ's people to help David.

One of Russ's men went in the ambulance with Paulie and called Russ. The agents already notified Ray. Russ called Lou to tell him everything. Charlie was there. Lou called Paulie's parents and told them they were on the way to the hospital. Shelley and Peter would follow. Allie, Molly, and Maria got into the limo, and they all left for the hospital. Ray told Lou a state trooper would meet him at the state line and escort them to the hospital. By the time Paulie got to the emergency room, he had lost a lot of blood. His left lung was collapsed. On the way to the emergency room, the Paramedic put a needle through Paulie's chest wall to relieve the internal pressure. If not for his quick thinking, Paulie would have died in the ambulance. When he got to the emergency room, they quickly started giving him blood and put in a chest tube. A chest tube is something that is inserted between the ribs and into the chest cavity to get out the blood and equalize the pressure so the lung would inflate. It worked, but it's only a quick fix. Paulie was still bleeding inside. If he was to survive, he had to be rushed to surgery to get the bullet out and stop the bleeding. Ray had already gotten to the hospital, and the driver of the van and the shooters were in custody. Ray called Lou and brought them up to speed. He told them Paulie was alive and in surgery, but critical.

Ray asked how they knew Paulie was there. The shooters did not mention they saw Paulie with Junior. They were eager to make a deal. They said Rivera heard that someone saw Paulie in town. The word came down to "WACK" him. When they saw Paulie driving out of town, they called Rivera, and he gave the okay for the hit. They followed him, and when they had the chance, they did their deed. They were willing to plead guilty to a lesser charge in exchange for testifying against Rivera. When the attorney told this to Ray, ray informed him only if Paulie did not die. If Paulie died, they would have to testify against Rivera. They would be charged with murder one. If they cooperated, the government would not ask for the death penalty. They were caught dead to rights. They had no choice but to deal. Paulie was in surgery for six hours. Everyone had gotten there before he was out of surgery. Maria was a wreck. Everyone was. Paulie became like family to them. If Paulie died, it would be like losing a son. The town priest called Lou and offered a prayer. He told Lou he asked the local priest to come and sit with them. As they hung up, a young priest walked into the family room and introduced himself. He informed Lou that he would stay with them. They all said a prayer together. About thirty minutes later, two nuns from the parish came in and brought them food. They also sat with them. This gesture was very comforting. About an hour later, the surgeon came out to speak with them.

He said, "Paulie is a tough man and is in recovery. It was touch and go for a while. Luckily, the bullet hit a rib, fractured it, bounced off, a made an opening in his left lung. The bullet also nicked an artery between the ribs, which was where the bleeding was coming from. The bullet was lodged in a difficult place to reach. For a while, we thought we would have to leave it in. We managed to repair his lung and the artery. We did remove the bullet. He will be in recovery for a while. He still had a breathing tube inserted, and they were keeping him sedated. After recovery, he will go to the trauma intensive care unit. We need to watch for infection and other things. You could go in for only a minute or two. It will be some time before he goes to the ICU. I suggest you go to your hotel and come back in the morning. We will call you if anything changes, but we do not plan to wake him up until sometime in the morning. He needs the rest now." They all wanted to stay.

The priest asked, "Do you have a place to stay?"

Lou replied, "Yes father. We can't thank you and your parish enough for all that you have done."

The priest replied, "We are all Gods' children. God will heal him now. You all need to get some rest to be strong when he wakes up. I will be back after mass tomorrow."

Lou asked, "Father, where is your church? We would like to attend mass tomorrow morning."

The priest gave him the address and mass times and said, "We look forward to seeing you in the morning. I will be saying that mass for him."

Ray was happy things went well and planned to stop by to see Paulie for a minute then wanted to get back to the office. He wanted to question the shooters. Everyone went in to see Paulie. When the girls saw him, they burst into tears. He was pale, and just looked lifeless. The recovery nurse was so nice but firm. She said they needed to control themselves. She explained what all the equipment was for and why he looked so pale.

She said, "As bad as you think he looks, he actually looks good. He is doing better than expected." As she was leaving the room, she said, "I can only give you five minutes. I have a lot to do for him before he goes to the ICU."

They thanked her for her kindness and understood. They all spoke to Paulie as if he were awake and could hear them. After almost ten minutes, the nurse came in and said they needed to leave. It was about seven-thirty at night. Her shift started at seven. She told them she would be his nurse until he went upstairs. They exchanged numbers, and she gave them the nurse's station number for the ICU. I will call you when they are transferring him. They left and headed back to the hotel.

David's pre-trial was in two days. Lou and Allie would leave late tomorrow afternoon. Maria and Molly would stay in town with Paulie's parents. When they arrived, Maria gave them the story. Once Paulie was stable, and there were no signs of infection, they would have him transferred to the hospital back home. The doctor did say his recovery would take a few weeks. He may need some physical therapy to get his strength back. They all decided they would not tell David about any of this. Lou called Ray and Russell and asked them not to say a word to David about this. Everyone was tired. It was a stressful day. They ordered room service and had a bite to eat.

Meanwhile, Ray was interrogating the shooters. There was a great deal of planning that needed to go into the bust for next Saturday night. Ray did not know how to contact Junior and hoped Junior did not find out about this for fear he would back out. They had his picture and knew what he looked like. They could protect him during the raid. Even if Junior heard of this, it probably would not change Rivera's plan. In fact, it might make him feel more secure. As much as he wanted to have Rivera picked up for this, he knew he had to wait. To catch him with the product, and add these charges, would put him away for life. He did not want to make a deal with him unless he could provide them with a great deal of significant information. Part of this was personal because Paulie was his friend as well. He wanted Rivera to fry for this. A couple of hours later, Paulie's nurse called to let them know he was being taken upstairs.

She said, "His nurse is a friend of mine. I spoke to her. She will call you after he is settled in. Don't worry. He is still doing fine, and with the blood they gave him, his color was starting to come back. About two hours later, his ICU nurse called and said Paulie was doing fine.

Lou asked, "I have to leave tomorrow afternoon. What time do you think they will try to wake him up?"

She replied, "I won't be here, but my friend Denise is my relief. She will be here. If he has a good night, they plan on removing the breathing tube around ten in the morning, and start to reduce the sedation."

Lou thanked her said, "We will get there around nine. After you wake him up, he will want to see familiar faces."

She replied, "I understand. I will let Denise know, and she will call you if there are any changes."

They had already spoken with David earlier and did not tell him anything. Lou knew that was the right thing to do. This would drive David crazy if he knew and could not be there for Paulie. Everyone was exhausted and decided to get some sleep. Molly and Allie stayed up for a short time.

Molly said to Allie, "Baby, I know I've asked this before, and I love being like your mom, but do you want us to try to find her now since you are pregnant again?"

Allie replied in a stern tone, "ABSOLUTELY NOT! You all are my family." They went to sleep.

Morning came, and everyone was at the hospital at nine. They all went to early mass. Everything went as planned. Paulie woke up without a problem and was happy to see everyone there. He spoke to Lou privately after spending some time with Maria first, then the family. He told Lou everything. Lou explained that he would be transferred home when his strength was back, and there were no signs of infection. That made Paulie happy. Everyone stayed for the day, and then Allie and Lou left to head back home.

CHAPTER 10

IT'S ALL ABOUT TIMING

It was Monday morning. Lou and Allie arrived at the courthouse and met with David's attorney before court convened. Lou filled Mike in on everything that happened and made sure he did not tell David about Paulie being shot. With all these new possibilities, which were still unclear, along with the forensic evidence, which was not completed, everyone knew David would be held over for trial. Mike would ask for a continuance. He wanted more time to gather their findings. David was brought into the courtroom and sat between Lou and Mike. Allie was in the first row right behind him. Everyone stood as the judge entered the courtroom. When the court convened, the judge brought the court to order. The defense made a motion for a continuance to complete their investigation.

The judge asked, "Does the prosecution feel they have enough evidence to proceed?"

The prosecution stated, "Yes your honor."

The judge stated, "Motion for continuance denied. The defense will have plenty of time to compile any evidence if this case goes to trial. The prosecution can proceed."

The prosecution presented all the evidence they had against David. It was all concrete evidence. They rested their case. The defense presented what they had so far, which was mostly circumstantial evidence. They rested their case. The judge reminded everyone that this was just a preliminary trial to determine if there was enough evidence to take the case to trial. The judge ruled that the case would go to trial. Due to the sensitive nature of the case and the deceased, jury selection would start on Wednesday. The trial date was set for a week from today unless a jury could not be agreed upon in time. David's attorney asked if David could visit with his wife who is pregnant, for 30 minutes before the Marshals return him to his place of holding. The judge granted that request. David and Allie met in a room. David assured Allie that everything would be okay. He had full faith that Russell's team would find something.

Allie asked, "How are you doing babe?"

"I'm fine. How is the baby, and the business going? Are you feeling alright?"

Allie replied, "Everyone is fine. Besides some morning sickness, I'm doing okay."

They were not allowed to have physical contact. David didn't care. He kissed and hugged Allie until the Marshal came in and reminded them that was not allowed. It seemed like seconds, and their time was up. They were grateful that they had some time together. The Marshall took David away. Allie started to cry after he left. She did not want David to see how upset she was. This case was now in the hands of timing. Allie and Lou started for home. They called to check on Paulie. He was awake, in pain, but doing fine. The doctors said he was very lucky and should make a full recovery. Many things were starting to develop.

*****

It was now Wednesday, and the results came back from the particulates found in David's truck. In the locking mechanism, they found a fiber. Since they had many items of clothing obtained from their warrant when they searched Rivera's house, it matched a jacket that they had in evidence. That placed him in the trunk of David's car. However, all of this was still not enough as compared to the evidence the government had against David. It could be enough to prove reasonable doubt, but they did not want to run that risk. Thousands of those jackets were probably made. For this evidence to be concrete, they somehow had to tie it to some form of DNA match. There had to be more.

On Friday, the jury selection was completed. The trial would begin on Monday. Ray spent all week planning the bust for Saturday night. Without Paulie, they had no idea whether the drug deal was still on. Ray was building quite the case against Rivera, especially with the statements from the shooters. He wanted this bust. That was why he did not pick up Rivera for ordering the hit on Paulie. He wanted to have as many charges against him as possible. He wanted a case so strong, he would not have to make any deals. Two trials were in progress for the Florida and Connecticut crime bosses. Both were going well. Ray's junior attorneys were handling those. They were clear-cut cases. Once the IRS added their charges, it was just a matter of connecting the dots to get a conviction. Ray was always available for a conference if needed. They spoke each day after court. Everyone was fully updated on their progress. Vincent's trial would be last. They had so much evidence and IRS findings that they did not need Rivera to put him away.

Ray was obsessed with Rivera. Besides the pressure from above, Max was his friend. Ray was having a hard time trying to keep his emotions out of this. Paulie was doing well and would be transferred to the hospital back home on Sunday. When Mike, Ray, Russell, and Lou had their weekly conference call on Friday, they decided they would have to tell David about Paulie. They knew he would ask why Paulie was not in the courtroom during the trial. Lou decided to tell David when they spoke Friday night. When they spoke, David was devastated. He called the hospital to speak with Paulie. There was still critical missing pieces that were required to get David's charges dropped, especially if Rivera did not confess. They also did not know what information Junior had regarding David. That Friday, they received a call from the court clerk informing them the judge was ill, and the trial would not start until Wednesday. In a way, this was a blessing. It gave them more time.

The hospital gave Paulie his cell phone. They did not want him to have it at first. They did not want him to be stressed. He needed to rest. He saw multiple messages from Junior. He called Ray to see if there were any changes. He wanted Ray to know Junior had been trying to contact him. Paulie said, "I'll call him and get back to you."

Paulie called Junior it went to voicemail. He left a message for him to call back. Early that evening, Junior returned his call. He was frantic because he had not been able to reach Paulie. He heard what happened and feared the worst. Paulie filled him in asked if it was still on for Saturday night. Junior told him it was but the time was changed to two am, but the location was the same. Junior asked, "I'm I square with the feds?"

Paulie replied, "It's all taken care of. After the bust, Ray, the prosecutor, will meet with you to go over the details of how it works. Junior, you have to tell me what you know about David. Don't change your mind. Do the right thing and enjoy a good life."

Junior said, "I don't have a lot of time. I spoke to Johnny. I have the book on the judge. It shows dates, bets, everything. You are going to have to trust me because I have no way of getting it to you, I can fill you in on David Saturday night. I have to go now."

Paulie said, "I trust you, but we can't do a thing on your word. To have this Judge removed from the case, I need that book. I can have someone call you. His name is Russell. He will set it up to get it from you. You can trust him. I have many times."

Junior said, "Okay, I'll wait for his call."

Paulie's nurses were pissed that he was spending this much time on the phone. They wanted to take it back. Paulie explained, "You have no idea how important this is. This is why I'm here. Please, let it be."

His nurse said, "As long as you don't get upset and excited, and your vital signs stay normal, you can keep your phone. Any changes and we are taking the phone." Paulie agreed.

Maria had taken the week off from work and was there every day. Molly had gone home once Paulie was out of the woods. Maria said, "Don't worry. I'll kick his ass if he doesn't listen."

Paulie immediately called Ray and filled him in on the change. He asked Ray to set up a conference call with Russ, Lou, and Mike. Ray said, "I'll do it now and call you right back."

A few minutes passed, and Ray called back. Paulie explained everything to them. The time change for Saturday night was not a problem. He would have agents placed and hidden well in advance, as well as others standing by. Russell explained he would call Junior and get the information from him. This information is what Mike and Ray would need to get this judge off the case. Saturday night the additional information Junior supplied regarding David would help Mike's case.

*****

It was Saturday night. It was time to put everything into motion. Ray wanted the agents there early. Before any of the drug dealers arrived. He knew they would probably have some people there early as well. The area was being monitored by drones. Ray's agents had to be there first. This would be a large bust. No one went to sleep Saturday night. They were all up waiting to hear how it went. At about one-thirty am, some cars showed up. They lined up against each other. Everyone stayed in their cars until ten of two, when two SUV's arrived. One went to one side, the other went to the other side. Everyone exited the cars. They were heavily armed. Ray had four snipers on overwatch. The drones identified snipers that were on other rooftops. The drones were a great help. They also had men hiding in machinery on the dock. The local police were standing by outside the entrance to the dock in unmarked cars. This could easily become a bloodbath. In the distance were two FBI helicopters that were ready to enter the scene when needed. This was a large operation.

The drones by were equipped with thermal and infrared cameras, they counted twelve heavily armed men, fourteen including Rivera and the supplier, and six snipers performing overwatch. Ray made it perfectly clear he wanted Rivera alive. When the merchandise and money were being checked, Ray gave the go sign. The snipers immediately took out the other snipers. As set of agent approached and identified themselves, shots rang out. The FBI snipers took out some of those on the ground as well. The helicopters and the police that were standing by arrived. In no time, the buyers and dealers were surrounded. Junior slid under one of the trucks. In seconds, the FBI snipers took out eight men. Rivera and the supplier tried to get to their cars and run. They had nowhere to go. The local police had barracked them in with their cars and a tactical vehicle. The remaining men, including Junior, dropped their weapons and surrendered. The agents took them into custody. It was over in less than fifteen minutes. Rivera was alive, and they confiscated over a 20 million dollars in street value of cocaine and heroin. A van pulled up to take those who surrendered to jail. Medical vehicles arrived to tend to those that were wounded and still alive. Rivera and the supplier were taken in two separate cars to the FBI field office. Upon Ray's return to the office, they already had Junior separated and waiting. Ray wanted to meet and speak with him first. Junior had much to tell. He got the book on the judge to Russell. Ray had not spoken with Russ yet regarding the contents.

Junior explained that Rivera had set up David on the orders from Vincent, and on Vincent's orders, Rivera killed Max. However, there were no recordings of these conversations. Therefore, it could be all considered hearsay evidence and not admissible. Ray feared he would have to make a deal with Rivera to get a confession and confirm this. Junior did his part. Ray would get him into the program after the trial. Ray took a minute to call Russ and Lou by conference call. He filled them in but explained; it was far from over. It was great information and a great bust. However, to make it rock solid, he would need a confession. Ray felt if Rivera did not confess, he could possibly make it stick with Junior's testimony, especially if other facts they might turn up can be tied together. This was one huge puzzle. Ray had to make all the pieces fit. He could not talk long and told them they would speak tomorrow and decide on what to do about the judge.

It was late. Everyone was exhausted. Ray decided to let Rivera stew a bit. He would get some sleep and start fresh in the morning. Molly, Lou, and Allie were very upset. They had hoped this would be it and David would not have to go to trial. In their eyes, everything was getting so confusing. What evidence was good, what was questionable, what might be admissible, and what may not? Lou's was not a criminal defense attorney. He did not have David there to help sort this out. Even he was getting confused as to what this all meant. Mike called a few minutes later and apologized for calling so late. He let them know he heard about the bust from Ray. He thought this was great news. Lou put him on speaker and asked him to sum this all up.

Lou said, "Mike, everything is just appearing to be a mess of information. We are all confused. What does it all mean?"

Mike replied, "I understand. There is quite a bit of information here, and much is in bits and pieces. Let me simplify it for you. First, you need to understand the process. Proving innocence beyond any reasonable doubt is always the best method. However, proving enough reasonable doubt to get an acquittal is just as good. Let's talk about what we know so far. The FBI has a strong case with evidence. They have David's knife with his prints and DNA on it. They can prove that was the murder weapon. They have a witness who will testify that she saw Max and David arguing earlier that day. David has no alibi for the time of the murder. They have fibers from David's trunk on the deceased, and in the white van. They a match to the flooring of the garage where David's car was parked on the plastic bag Max was wrapped in and the van. The FBI also has proof that the murder scene was in the garage where David's car was parked. They also have a fax payment from David for the rental of the van which was also in his name."

Lou interrupted and said, "Sounds like they have a guaranteed conviction if you ask me."

Mike said, "So it appears. Things are not always as they appear. Let's look at what we have so far. In creating a timeline from when David made his last purchase until the time he spoke with Paulie, he did have time to commit the murder and move the body to the vacant building. However, there is nothing on the traffic cameras that day that shows the van. If David had tried to avoid cameras and take the side streets, there would not have been enough time due to the additional travel time. We also have fibers from Rivera's jacket from both the garage support and David's trunk. We also have a match to the dust on the garage floor to the dust on the bottom of Rivera's shoes. Although circumstantial, even the video shows a man walking towards David's car that is obscured when he passes the garage support. It's in black and white, and not clear enough to say the jacket the person is wearing matches the fiber from Rivera's jacket found in David's trunk.

The FBI will argue that the fiber could have gotten there the day he approached David on the highway. The question still remains, if nothing further develops, was this enough to place reasonable doubt in a jury's mind? Russ's team is still going through David's trunk. If we could get one piece of DNA that belongs to Rivera, we have a chance. We still have to see what comes from Junior's statement and Rivera's interrogation today. The trial starts on Wednesday. We still have to see what is on the book that Russell received from Junior on this judge. We have a few days to see how the rest pans out. For now, try not to worry. Get some sleep. Let's wait to hear from Ray tomorrow. His agents are getting Junior's statement tonight, and those of the shooters. From what I understand, they have rolled over on Rivera. They confirmed that Rivera authorized the hit on Paulie. This gives Ray a huge advantage. Taking into account whatever he gets from Junior, he may be able to get a confession from Rivera. I know he does not want to make a deal with Rivera. I do not believe he does not want David to go to prison either. He will do the right thing."

Lou said, "Thanks for the call and the explanation. We are to close to this. It's hard to think straight."

Mike replied, "That's why you hired me. By the way, I just got back from seeing David and letting him know all of this. His spirits are great. Actually, he is more worried about all of you. Get some rest. Goodnight."

Everyone was feeling more positive, hoping between Russ and the interviews, everything would come together. Ray had the ball in his court. He was good at his job. If anyone could pull this off, he could. No matter how the truth comes out, if Ray could prove Rivera killed Max. That carries the death penalty. Doing life in prison is better than dying by lethal injection any day. As anxious as everyone was, they all went to sleep. Allie and Molly interviewed and hired the two additional people this week. A lot was going on with the business. As hard as this was, everything else had to continue. It was good therapy and helped to keep their minds occupied. Even for a few moments. The shop and spa in town virtually ran itself, and Julia was doing an outstanding job of running it. The Paris fashion show was only a month away, and the Allie M. line would be introduced to Paris at that show. Allie and Molly really needed to be there. At worse, they could send the girls in advance to get everything set up, and they would just fly the day before the show, and leave the next after. That would depend on the trial. The timing could not have been any worse. Paulie was being transferred to the hospital back home in the morning. That would make things easier for Maria who was still in the city. Her job was very understanding and gave her as much time off as she needed. She spoke with her assistant daily. The hotel was still under construction. Besides deadlines to complete certain aspects of the project, there really was not too much to worry about. Everything was on schedule. If all went well, Paulie would be out of the hospital in two weeks and be able to go home. He was up and moving around, but still did not have all his strength back. That would take time and some physical therapy.

On Sunday morning, the family went to mass as always. At brunch, everyone asked about David. This made it quite difficult and even a bit uncomfortable for them. They knew everyone was genuinely concerned. Everyone knew the trial was starting on Wednesday. Lou had finished a large contract for one of his clients, which they approved. His junior attorneys could handle it from that point forward. His office manager had everything else under control. They hoped the trial would not go long before all of this additional information came together. The rest of the day was uneventful. About four o'clock, Lou's doorbell rang. Some of the townswomen stopped by to bring over food so Molly and Allie would not have to cook. They came in and chatted for a short time until Lou's phone rang. It was Ray. He had Russ and Mike on a conference call. Everyone left to give them privacy to talk. Lou put it on the conference phone in his office at home. This way, everyone could hear the conversation.

Mike started, "Russ, why don't you give us an update."

Russ replied, "We found a particulate on the edge of the weather stripping in David's trunk. It was actually wedged between the weather stripping and the metal. The metal appeared like a screw had been drilled through it at some point."

Lou replied, "Yes. David used to keep a police scanner in his car. He had one of those lift and lay mounts bolted to the trunk. When he got bored with it, he removed it."

"Well, we are trying to determine what it is. It could be dried skin, and there is an extremely small amount of dried blood there as well. Everyone missed it the first time because it was such a small amount. We got lucky and found it when we were going over the car again. It is too small for my equipment. I had to send it out to be analyzed. I used this lab before and told them I needed this rushed, no matter what the cost. They said it would be a minimum of at least three to five days. That is really it." Mike thanked him and turned it over to Ray.

Ray explained, "Initially, the shooters wouldn't talk. They had their lawyer present. They were being charged with attempted murder and various other charges. Combined, that could carry up to fifteen to twenty years if they survived. If anyone thought they talked, they would not last long on the streets. If they chose to cooperate and in consideration of their testimony, we would get rid of the minor charges and reduced the attempted murder charge to felony assault. That would carry five years with a chance for early parole and probation. They wanted the program, I said no. My boss would not approve it. They took the deal. This confirmed that Rivera ordered the hit on Paulie. I got their cell phone records. They showed a call from Rivera to them just minutes before they shot Paulie. I did not like reducing the charges, but if it leads to getting David off, and Rivera pinned to the wall, it is worth it. If they survived prison, it would be a miracle. Let me grab a coffee; I'll be right back." Everyone thought this was promising news. When Ray returned, he continued.

Ray added, "Junior was all set. He was approved for the program. This bust was huge. He also made a statement and agreed to testify that Rivera personally killed Max. He provided us with the full details of how, when and where. How the knife was gotten from David's car and how the van was rented. As it turns out, the last place David shopped, the clerk was on Vincent's parole. He was an addict. That's how they got David's credit card number."

Everyone was excited. This meant David's charges would be dismissed. Ray went on to add, "Don't get excited. Anthony is actually prosecuting David's case. He is on our side. However, the brass is not. At this time, they feel the case against David is airtight. Don't forget, they are also under pressure. It's one person's word against another. It has to be put together and must be rock solid. Since that hasn't been done yet, there is no proof to back it up. That makes it an easy case to lose. They are still going with the sure thing unless I can either break Rivera, get a confession, or you come up with evidence that is more conclusive. However, Junior gave us one additional thing. Paulie's friend Johnny came through. Russ, why don't you take it from here?"

Russ said, "You all know Junior got his hands on the book on the judge. I received it from him. This judge is corrupt as they come. I pulled everything on him. I have his financials and his case histories. The numbers don't match. He does not make or have enough in investments to have everything he owns. He has offshore accounts and a history of dismissing cases that involved the crime organizations. That is why he was so pissed when Ray got the other judge to sign the warrants. I gave it all to Ray."

Ray added, "I took a big chance, one that could end my career if it backfired. Without telling my boss, I tried to contact him. He is not sick. He is in Florida playing golf. I left a message for him to call me. He called this morning. I did a stupid thing, but it worked and paid off. I told him everything I had on him. Of course, he denied it. Then I gave him account numbers, bookie names, and other information. He asked me what I wanted. I told him two things. First, remove yourself from this case. Second, retire. I told him. Personally, I don't give a shit what you did. David is my friend, and Max was like family. You need to make it right. He said, and if I don't? I told him I would let it all out and arrest him. He said, and if I do this? I told him no one would ever find out what I had. He said you know your career is over. I told him to let it go. I still had the information and could always use it. He asked how do I know you won't use it later? I told him, do the right thing so I won't have to. Let's call it my insurance policy. Two hours later I received a call that the judge had decided to retire, and removed himself from the case. We now have a new judge. I know him. He is a fair man and is only interested in the truth, and justice.

You could hear a pin drop in the room. It was completely silent for a moment. Mike said, "Ray, you have balls."

Ray went on to say, "Let's forget that now and move on to Rivera. He's playing hardball. He wants the program. I'm sorry, but I won't give it to him. Max was to close to me. Mike, you may have to earn your money."

Mike replied, "No problem. Who can blame you? Especially after all you've done."

Ray replied, "I won't stop working on him. Don't worry. With his record, the hit on Paulie, this drug bust, and Junior's statement on Max, he will never see daylight as a free man again. He thinks we are bluffing. I also charged him with Max's murder. That puts the death penalty on the table. If David is convicted, he has to gamble that I can't tie him to David. I believe I could. I am letting him, and his attorney, sit on this for a while. Mike, I hope you understand that regardless of what Anthony thinks, he has to do his job, so don't take it personally."

Mike and everyone agreed, "We understand."

Ray said, "Unless something changes, I'll see you all on Wednesday."

After they ended the call, Russ and Mike stayed on the line. Mike said, "I want you all to relax. I will make this happen. I am that good. If Russ's findings come back in our favor, that will help even more, and if Rivera breaks, we're home free." Everyone thanked each other and ended the call. This was the first real sign of hope they had. It still could be touch and go. If both or either of the last two things play out, David's charges would be dropped. They all were thinking. Thankfully, Ray was a good man and attorney. As much as Max was his friend, which was his driving force, he believed in David. He cared about the truth and justice. Everyone had to wait now. About a half an hour later, David called. He had already spoken with Mike and knew all the details.

Allie said, "I love you and miss you so much."

David replied, "I love you too. Don't worry, this will all work out. We have the best people working on it. Let me say hi to the baby." Allie put the phone next to the baby's ear as David was talking to him. The baby was laughing. He knew his father's voice.

Allie took the phone back. She wanted to lift his spirits. As good as he sounded, she knew him. Most of this was a front so they wouldn't worry. "Babe, every night we talk, you never ask me what I'm wearing when I'm in bed."

David replied, "You're really going to do this to me now?"

Allie just laughed and said, "I know you'll be home soon. Know that I'll be waiting."

David replied, "That's good to know."

Allie said, "Babe, I know you'll be home soon. I can feel it. Don't give up."

David said, "I'll never give up. I hope you are right. Now go get some rest. You're sleeping for two you know."

After they hung up, everyone relaxed. Molly and Lou had some wine. Allie was not drinking alcohol because she was pregnant. She had water. Earlier, they stopped by the hospital to spent time with Paulie. He looked great and was anxious to get out of the hospital and go home. He was walking around the floor, and sitting in the chair. Maria stopped by to say hi and thank them for stopping in to see Paulie. He insisted on her sleeping home tonight. The doctors at the hospital told him he would start PT tomorrow. If all went well, they would release him after a couple of days and have a home nurse continue his PT.

Lou said, "I don't want to put the cart before the horse, but we have to plan a welcome home and welcome back party for Paulie and David."

Allie, Molly, and Maria responded, "We have already thought of that."

Everyone laughed and spent some time together. Maris was tired. Allie told her just to spend the night at her house. She would enjoy the company.

CHAPTER 11

CAN THEY PULL IT OFF?

Today would probably be the last day of testimony in the trials of the Connecticut and Florida bosses before it went to the jury. Those cases and Vincent's case were rock solid. His trial would start right after David's case was done. Keep in mind they were waiting to start Vincent's trial so any additional information found could be added to the charges. The corrupt federal judge was the lucky one. He got away free and clear. Ray looked at that as a small price to pay to put these people away for good. This would really shake up the East Coast families. Ray was around for a long time. He knew people within these organizations would have much to answer for. However, in a short time, business would get back to normal. It's a vicious cycle. He wanted this promotion. After all these years, this was starting to wear on him. He put many in jail just for others to take their place. Does it ever end? The process would start all over again from the beginning. It was time for him to place these responsibilities into the hands of younger and upcoming attorneys.

Over the years, Ray missed a great deal of time with his wife many things while his children were growing up. He wanted some quality time with them now. He had grandchildren he rarely saw, except on holidays. He had another grandchild on the way. Ray's father was a retired federal prosecutor. He died a couple of years ago from a heart attack. Ray never forgot what his father told him. He said, *"Ray, No matter how much you love what you do, if you do it long enough, it will take its toll on you on consuming your life."* Ray's father was right. Ray had been feeling it for some time now. His boss, the Regional Director, was retiring in three months. Ray knew if he won all these cases, he would be a shoo-in for that job. If he got the position, he would rarely have to be in court. He would now be the one in charge of budgets and approving deals. If Ray were lucky enough to have a great staff of attorneys as his boss does, this would be a great job to have for the remainder of his career. Ray's wife was always supportive of him, but she was hoping for this as well. He would not have to work weekends or holidays and have time for his family.

No one knew how many friends Lou actually made over the years, or the many favors he did for others. When the time came, Lou would do whatever he could to help Lou get that position. The recommendation from Ray's boss would carry a lot of weight. What no one knew was, Ray's boss and Lou went to Law school together and were very good friends. Lou actually handled some real estate investments for him. In three months, his federal pension would max out. There was no reason for him to stay on with the FBI. Like Ray, he sacrificed for many years to make it to that position. He was too young for social security; however, between his pension and his investments, he could retire. He always joked with Lou about hiring him part-time. He wanted to keep active. He liked doing contract and real estate law. Only two or three days a week to keep him occupied. Lou would certainly do this. With David being a partner now, their firm grew by almost twenty-five percent in a short period. Lou could always use the extra help, and money was not an issue.

*****

Monday and Tuesday flew by. Tomorrow the trial would start. Russ had still not received the results from the lab, and Rivera was not budging. Ray could not get him to confess and turn against the organization. Lou had more than one opportunity to become a judge. Something he almost did once. However, his firm was started by his father. It was his father's legacy. He did not want to give that up. Even now with David on board, if he wanted to become a judge, he would have to leave the firm. There really was not a need for that. Lou had many attorneys working at the firm. He was only handling his three biggest clients. He worked less than if he were a judge, and made far more money. He was quite content with the way it worked out.

Wednesday morning everyone was in the courtroom. After all the formalities were over, David pleaded not guilty. Anthony and Michael made their opening statements to the jury. Anthony, the federal prosecutor, started to present the government's case. Ray reminded them not to take it personally because Anthony had a job to do. Anthony came out like a bull out of the starting gate. He was clearly trying to place a permanent impression in the minds of the jury. He called witness after witness. Cited test after test. Each time, adding one more nail to David's coffin. Ray told them Anthony had a reputation for going for the throat and was tough. He was certainly that and more. Mike did what he could to dismiss, or at least put a question in the jury's mind, for most things, but not all, especially the important ones. At the end of the first day, everyone felt like David would be convicted.

Mike told them, "Don't lose faith now. We will have our turn at bat. Honestly, he's screwing up and doesn't realize it."

Lou asked, "Why is that. Hell if I were on the jury, I would vote guilty today."

Mike replied, "David and I have been conferring all day. No offense Lou, thank God it's not you on the jury. Anthony is playing all his cards at the beginning. How much do you think the jury will remember by the time we present our case? Besides some minor things, he has nothing left. He showed all his cards except for one."

Lou asked, "What's that?"

Mike replied, "THE JOKER. Go have dinner. I have some things to prepare for tomorrow, and for God's sake, don't worry."

Lou did not know that Russ had given Mike the information on the prosecution's witness. Mike knew she was not scheduled to testify until the second day. She would be their first witness. The results came back on the dried skin and blood. They were correct. That is exactly what it was. However, due to the age and degradation of the small piece of tissue, it only came back at an 88% possible match for Rivera; however, the blood was a 100% match for Rivera. That was what Mike was hoping for and needed. The 88% could be disputed by Anthony, but not the blood. Together, it would be easy for Mike to show the jury they came from the same person. Mike had two choices now. He called Lou and Ray to discuss this.

Lou said, "Let's get the recess and present what we have and get these charges dropped."

Ray interrupted and said, "Lou. Don't take this wrong. We need to look at the larger picture.

"Do we," Lou replied.

(Ray paused), "Listen to me. I sound like I am part of the defense team. (He laughed). Do you want to show your hand right now? It's clear that the charges against David will be dropped. Now I need a favor. Does one or two more days make that much of a difference? I need you to let Mike do his job. I want to nail the coffin shut on Rivera. Once Mike does what he needs to do, and we go into chambers with the judge, Rivera's attorney is not going to know what we have. Some of this evidence cannot be presented to the jury yet. If Rivera's attorney gets his hands on this, it could hurt the chances of getting Rivera to roll over. This information is what I need to get Rivera to confess. If his attorney warns him of it, he will have time to come up with a story. I have to catch him off guard. This is how it could play out, and I might ask Anthony to suggest this. Let's not have the judge not drop the charges yet. Request a two-day recess to give everyone time to check out the newly presented evidence. Trust me, Rivera's attorney will run to talk with his client, especially not knowing exactly what we have. I will be there to hammer in the nail. Lou, please, just two more days. Let's not let David's time away from his family be in vain."

Lou asked, "Have you discussed this with David?"

Mike replied, "I did. He agrees. It's only two or three more days." After careful thought, Lou agreed.

Molly was furious. She did something she has never done. She started yelling at Lou. "I WANT MY SON HOME. I WANT MY SON HOME NOW. WHAT IN THE HELL IS WRONG WITH YOU? WHAT ARE YOU DOING?"

Allie hugged Molly who was crying, "Mom, if this is what David wants, then this is what I want. Don't be mad at dad. That is why he agrees, for David."

Molly still crying went over to Lou. "Baby, I am so sorry. You are right. Can you forgive me?"

Lou replied, "There's nothing to forgive. Saying no was my first thought as well. I knew this is what David would want. Stop crying. Our son will be home soon."

Molly, holding Lou, said to Allie, "Baby, that's the first time you have called us mom and dad at the same time. We both love you." Allie just smiled and replied, "Because you are."

Everyone was very emotional. No one thought to ask Russell what information he found out about the witness. They would find out in the morning. What they needed now, was some family time. Russ ended the conversation by saying, "I will be there in the morning with all the documentation. Everyone, we are doing the right thing. Think about David being home for the weekend. Goodnight." Allie, Lou, and Molly stop by to visit David for a moment. They did not discuss the case. They were just happy to see him. He looked strong but weathered. They could tell he could not wait for this to end.

The next day court convened at ten o'clock sharp. Ray had met with Anthony well before court started to discuss his plan. Anthony agreed to go along with it. As tough as he was, like Ray, he believed in justice and finding the truth, especially after seeing the documentation on his first witness. They decided to call her, then request a recess. David knew most of this. He did not know how they were going to play it. Anthony still needed to play hardball. He called his first witness. This girl stated she witnessed David and Max arguing before the time he was murdered. Just as Anthony called for the witness, the courtroom doors opened. Everyone turned. Maria was wheeling Paulie in the courtroom a wheelchair. No one had any idea he was coming. David started to have tears running down his face and stood up. Two Federal Marshals immediately grabbed him. David was strong. They could not get him back in the chair. One of the Marshals drew his Taser.

Mike immediately yelled, "EVERYONE, PLEASE, CALM DOWN. DAVID, SIT DOWN!" David sat. Mike apologized to the court and the jury. He stated, "Your honor, the man that was just wheeled in is the defendant's best friend. They grew up together. He was ambushed and shot while obtaining information for this case. He was recently transferred home two days ago. He has not seen my client since the incident. If the prosecution and the court do not object, can he come forward momentarily to see the defendant?"

The judge asked, "Does the prosecution have any objections. Anthony did not. The judge asked the Marshals to check the visitor and escort him to see the defendant. The judge stated to David, "Sir, do not take this as a sign that this court is weak. However, this court does have compassion, but I warn you. Any further outbreaks of that nature and I will have you place in shackles for the remainder of this trial. Am I perfectly clear?"

David replied, "Yes your honor. I apologize to the court, guests, and the jury. It will not happen again."

The Marshals patted down Paulie. Maria wheeled Paulie to the front to see David. When she placed the wheelchair next to David, he did not stand. Both Marshals were on each side of the wheelchair. David leaned over to hug Paulie. Not a word was said. They both cried. This was only a brief moment, and the judge instructed Maria to return Paulie to the seating area.

The judge asked, Is the prosecution and the defense prepared to continue?" They both responded, "Yes your honor."

The judge told Anthony, "Call your next witness."

Toni Angelina was called. She was a girl in her thirties. Before she entered the witness stand, she was sworn in. The clerk asked her to state her name for the record. She complied.

Anthony asked, "Ms. Angelina, did you witness an argument between the defendant and the deceased on the day the crime was allegedly committed?"

"Yes."

Anthony asked, "Can you tell the court where you witnessed this argument?"

"I was coming out of the coffee shop across the street. I was walking towards the parking garage of the hotel on my way back to work. They were both standing just at the entrance to the parking garage and yelling at each other. I thought they were going to fight."

Mike stated, "Objection your honor. The witness is not qualified to make that determination, and the prosecution did not ask her for an opinion."

The judge said, "Sustained." He looked at Toni, "Ms. Angelina. I am instructing you to limit your answers to the question or questions asked."

"Yes your honor. I'm sorry."

Anthony then asked her, "In your opinion. Did you get the impression that they might end up in a fistfight?"

"Yes."

Anthony asked, "What did you do?"

"I got out of there as quickly as I could. I did not want to be involved."

Anthony asked her, "What do you do for a living?"

"I work as a secretary."

Anthony asked, "Are you married with children?"

"Yes, I have been married for ten years and have two children."

Anthony said, "No more questions your honor." The judge informed Mike he could proceed.

Mike walked up to her and asked, "Ms. Angelina, are you aware of the penalty for perjury."

"I think so."

Mike asked the judge if he could explain the penalties to the witness, or would the court prefer to.

The judge stated, "I will, thank you, counselor."

"Miss Angelina. Perjury means you willingly provided false statements or testimony under oath or by a signed statement. State and federal penalties for perjury include fines and/or prison terms upon conviction. Federal law (18 USC § 1621), for example, states that anyone found guilty of the crime will be fined or imprisoned for up to five years. Do you understand?"

The witness replied, "Yes your honor." However, Mike immediately noticed the new quiver in her voice. He knew he had her.

Mike asked, "Miss Angelina. Is this your real name or have you ever changed it other than when you were married?"

"Yes. I never changed my last name when I was married. This has always been my name."

Mike asked, "Can you point out the man you saw arguing with the deceased?" She pointed directly to David.

Mike asked, "Have you ever been involved in any way with anyone from a known criminal organization, such as gambling, prostitution, drugs?"

Anthony stood, "Objection your honor. Which question does the defense want to be answered? His question is not specific."

The judge responded, "Sustained. Rephrase your question counselor." Mike asked each question as separate questions. To each question, the witness responded no. Mike asked for a brief moment to confer with his client.

Mike asked the judge if he could approach the bench to have evidence admitted into the record. Mike knew exactly what Anthony would do.

Anthony immediately stood and stated, "Objection. The prosecution was not given this evidence during the discovery stage and has not had ample time to review it."

The judge said, "Sustained. You know better counselor."

Mike stated, "Your honor if it pleases the court, I am requesting a recess to meet in your chambers. A great deal of new evidence was just handed to me before the court convened. In the interest of not affecting another case, I would like for us to meet privately regarding this."

The judge was a bit perturbed by this. He asked, "If you received this new evidence before court went into session, why didn't you present it then, rather than have the prosecution call its first witness?"

Mike replied, "As you know your honor, the defendant has taken an active part as a member of his defense team. He was looking through this new evidence during the witness testimony and my cross-examination. When I asked for a brief moment to confer with my client, he was pointing out his findings. After reviewing the finding, this was the reason for my request."

The judge stated, "This is highly irregular. However, I will allow it if the prosecution has no objections." The prosecution did not object. Mike gambled that Anthony was also interested in the truth.

The judge stated, "Given these new developments, why don't we take an extended lunch? We will reconvene at one pm. Gentleman, please follow me to my chambers." The judge asked the bailiff to have lunch delivered to his chambers.

Lou, Mike, Ray, and Anthony, followed the judge to his chambers. When they were all seated, the judge said, "Okay Mike, show us what you have, and it better be good."

Mike stated, "Your honor, first let me take a minute to give you some background."

At that very moment, there was a knock on the door. The judge asked whomever it was to enter. It was his clerk. She apologized for the interruption, but there was an urgent call for Ray on line 1. Ray apologized and took the call. Covering the mouthpiece he said, the juries on both cases came back with a verdict. He was off the phone in less than two minutes.

He said, "I apologize, your honor. That was my office. The jury came back with a verdict on two large cases I handled. They wanted to inform me of the verdicts."

The judge asked, "Are these the two cases on the Connecticut and Vermont crime organizations?"

Ray replied, "Yes your honor."

The judge asked, "I have heard a great deal about them. So give us the news, from what I understand everyone in this room had a hand in them except for Anthony, and I'm sure he is curious as well."

Ray said, "In both cases, the jury voted the defendants were guilty on all counts. These men will be in prison for the rest of their lives. Sentencing is in three months."

Everyone shook Ray's hand and congratulated him. This was great news for him. Shortly after, a tray of sandwiches arrived. The judge said, "Let's talk while we eat. So let's have it, Mike."

Mike said, "That call was perfect timing your honor. As Ray and Anthony will verify, there is still the New York crime boss who has to go on trial. The outcome of this case could affect another case that hasn't gone to trial yet."

The judge asked, "Is that the third man from New York?"

Ray interjected and said, "Yes your honor. Mike, can I say a few words?"

Mike replied, "Of course."

Ray went on to say, "The government decided not to take that case to trial when this case came up. Although we will get the same verdict, we have a man in custody we cannot get to give us information." The judge asked, "Is that the Rivera man I've heard so much about?" Ray replied, yes your honor. In summary, we cannot get him to become a witness for the prosecution. He was the right-hand man of the boss. He took over the crime family when the boss was taken into custody. Rivera's attorney has been in court every day. We believe he is looking for information on this case to keep his client informed. This may seem highly irregular, but we had to pursue this case against David because of the way the evidence stacked up. However, we all know him, and none of us believed he committed the crime. We all believed he was set up because he would not represent Vincent, the crime boss from New York. He could not represent him due to a case he was involved with for a client who is now his wife. Due to a plea agreement, if David represented him, it would be a conflict of interest to that part of the government's agreement."

The judge asked, "Are you referring to the Allie Green case?"

Ray replied, "Yes."

The judge said, "Wait. Is the David in my court the same David that handled that case?"

Ray replied, "Yes your honor."

The judge replied, "Damn, the judge that was on that case is a personal friend of mine. He was telling me all about it. He said David was outstanding. Some of the best legal defense he has ever seen. I think I know where this is going. Continue please."

Ray said, Mike, let's show them the evidence."

They explained that the results of some skin and blood had just come back. It was a match for Rivera. It was obtained from David's trunk. They also showed him pictures of Toni Angelina, which was not her real name, at parties with these crime figures. They also had video from the barn in Vermont of her having sex with some of them. They provided the judge with all the documentation to show her identity was fake and showed him who she really was and her police record.

Ray went on to say, "Your honor, if we did this in court, I would lose my leverage to get Rivera to turn."

The judge asked, "If your case is so strong against this man from New York, why do you need Rivera?"

Ray replied, "Because if we can get him to turn, we might be able to clear up other crimes or murders. As we all know, the killing of an FBI agent carries the death penalty. A charge up to this point, he believes he can beat. With this evidence, we can use this as an advantage against him since he nor his attorney are aware that we have this."

The judge asked, "What is it you want the court to do."

Mike now took over and said, "Anthony will be asking for a two-day recess, so the government has time to review and evaluate the new evidence. We are asking for the court to grant that request. We believe Rivera's attorney will get back to his client. He will not know what the evidence is but will assume it has something to do with the testimony of Ms. Angelina. We believe she will confess that Mr. Rivera paid her to lie."

The judge replied, "You had this planned all along. I should throw you all out of my chambers. However, I think it is brilliant. I will grant this request under one condition. Come up with a means that allows me by law, to hold Ms. Angelina, or whatever her name is, in contempt of court for committing perjury. I hate when someone lies to my face. I have no problem dismissing the charges against David and sentencing her for perjury." Everyone agreed and finished lunch.

When court reconvened at one o'clock, Anthony requested that the cross-examination of Ms. Angelina be postponed. He requested a two-day recess for the government to review and re-evaluate this new evidence. The judge asked if the defense had any objections.

Mike replied, "The defense has no objection your honor providing we can recall Ms. Angelina and complete our cross-examination when we reconvene." The judge asked if the government agreed. Anthony agreed. The judge granted a two-day recess. Before the gavel struck, Rivera's attorney was out the door, and the trap was set. Ray called over to the lockup and asked them to contact him when Rivera's attorney arrives. Mike and Lou were informing

Russell and the family how the meeting with the judge went, and what was going on. David already knew. He was the one who originally devised this plan. The court would reconvene on Friday morning. If all went well, David could be home for the weekend.

*****

Meanwhile, everyone had two days. Ray, Anthony, and Mike would be wrapping it up from here if all went well. Allie and Molly had to leave for Paris next Thursday for the fashion show, which was on Saturday. They would fly back Sunday evening. Their staff would be leaving on Monday. They were sending the same models as well. They wanted their own models to show the line. They were laughing, if all went well, maybe Lou and David would join them, and they can stay a few extra days and make a mini-vacation of it. David and Allie had their actual honeymoon trip planned for February the following year. That was only six months away. In the meantime, Paulie found out that Johnny got of that group. Although he could not know where he went, he thought he would probably move to the mid-west to be closer to his sister. He was going to make a life for himself. Before he got involved with these people, he was one heck of a salesperson. He might try real estate. Junior got his deal with the government, and they would probably never see him again.

It was less than a half-an-hour before Ray heard from the agent at the lockup. Rivera's attorney arrived. Ray excused himself so he could go there. Ray informed everyone he would let them know of any new developments. They had two days, and things were looking promising. No one actually ate lunch and were hungry. Allie's morning sickness was gone. They decided to go out for an early dinner. Everything hinged on Rivera switching sides. It was not actually necessary to get David off. This new evidence would do that. The government still had a good case and a strong chance of getting a murder one conviction on Rivera for the murder of Max. This was about Ray. This was about getting so much on Vincent, and possibly solving many cold case murders. For Ray, it would tie the bow on him receiving the promotion when his boss retired. Russell. Molly, Allie, and Lou were discussing this at dinner. Molly still looked concerned. She was no happy that David was being used as a pawn, but she also could not forget that without Ray, Allie might not have gotten her verdict overturned, and might not be sitting with them tonight. She was very tormented and confused. Lou knew this. He could see it, as well as sense it. Allie was sitting on one side of him, and Molly on the other.

Lou gently placed a hand on each of their arms and said, "You don't have to say what you are feeling. I can see it in both your faces. On Friday, our son is coming home. I gave Ray his two days. We owed him that. David is our son. I will not allow this to go any further than that."

They both smiled. Lou knew the girls understood. Lou was a man of character and principal. He was as strong as they come. If he made that decision, that would happen. They did not know the connection Lou had to help Ray. If Ray was promoted, and Lou had any part of it happening, he would never want Ray to know. Sometimes certain things are best left unsaid. The rest of the night was quiet. Everyone was tired. When they got back to their hotel, they all went to bed. There were two messages for Allie. Lou's housekeeper was trying to reach her. Someone came to the house twice looking for her. She told Lou and Molly. If it were any of their staff, they would have called her. Who could this be, and what did it mean? It was late, and she did not want to call Lou's housekeeper. She would wait until tomorrow.

Everyone got a good night's sleep. Ray called about ten o'clock in the morning. Rivera's attorney stayed until ten o'clock the previous night. Ray had not heard anything. He was going to the lock-up now to see if anything further developed. Everyone had a day to try to unwind. The court was not due to go back into session until the following morning. Allie called Lou's housekeeper to see who it was that came looking for her. The only thing she could tell him was it was a man. Later that same day, a woman came by. They did not leave a business card or message. They only asked if Allie lived there. She told Allie she would not give them that information and asked them to leave. They left without giving her a problem. She also told Allie she reported this to the police. When she told Lou, Lou could access the door camera from his laptop and preview the previous footage. When he got to those times, Allie did not recognize either person or their voices. They were both very polite and promptly left when asked. Allie thought to herself, what now? Would this ever stop?

Since they had the day ahead of them, Allie and Molly went to do some shopping after breakfast. Allie was a thin girl and starting to show. When they got home, they would go to the doctor and find out if they were having a boy or a girl. They also wanted to visit with David. Lou, Mike, and Russell went to see David and then went to the lockup to spend time with Ray. David was surprised that Rivera had not wanted to make a deal yet. They had enough on him to ask for the death penalty. David wondered why he would risk that. In all his years as a criminal defense attorney, at the higher levels, there was honor among criminals. When the death penalty was on the table, all honor was gone. If you talked, you might be killed, if you did not, you would be still be killed. Making a deal was always the best choice. However, in this case, all Ray was willing to do was take the death penalty off the table. There would be no witness protection program for Rivera, not after killing Max. He would die in prison of old age. At some point, he would probably be killed in prison.

Lou took a few minutes to step outside. He wanted to call Ray's boss. When they were on the phone, they caught up a bit. Lou went on to tell him what a great job Ray did in all these cases. In the end, he would get convictions on all of them. Tom and Harry were also convicted of all charges. Harry was sentenced to ten years, with a chance for parole after seven. Tom, on the other hand, received seventy-five years for planning, and being an accessory to Jack's murder, along with all the IRS charges and smaller other charges. He would never see a day of freedom again. On the trip to his facility, he tried to escape. He got a gun away from an officer and was shot and killed in the process. This did not surprise anyone. Tom was too cocky. He could never spend his life behind bars. Only Vincent was left. He would surely die in prison.

After they chatted for a bit, he asked Lou, "Is this your pitch to ask me for a favor and help Ray get my job?"

Lou laughed and said, "There were always two things about you and I. First, I could never fool you in college, and second; I could never beat you on the golf course."

Ray's boss told Lou, "Not to worry my old friend. Ray will be offered my position. He has more than earned it. He is the best man for the job. Now I have a question for you."

Lou said, "Just ask."

He replied, "The wife and I are buying the old Morgan place outside of your town. It needs some work, but it was a steal. We both loved it in that area the few times we came to visit you. The golf course is fantastic, and the winter sports are great."

Lou replied, "That's great. Molly will be so happy to hear that. What can I do to help?"

"With my workload, can you handle the legal end for me and keep an eye on the workers. I hired the contractor you recommended a while back to get the place in shape. We want it ready when we move the late fall."

Lou replied, "Consider it done."

He asked, "There is one more thing."

Lou said, "Anything."

Ray's boss asked, "After we get settled in, do you think you have a spot for me two or three days a week. You know me. I can't sit still."

Lou replied, "There is no need to ask my friend. That was the first thing that came to my mind when you said you were moving to our area. I was going to ask you if you wanted some part-time work with the firm after you settled in. David is expanding the criminal-defense part of the firm. The way the town is developing, everything is growing fast. I can certainly hire new attorneys that eventually will get the experience, but they are wet behind the ears. I could really use your help."

Lou was a strategic man. He made Ray's boss feel like he was doing Lou a favor rather than the other way around. Lou was happy that Ray would get the job. Ray was so tense; he did not know whether he should tell him. He felt as if they owed Ray so much. Most prosecutors would have never allowed the cooperation that he and Anthony gave them on both Allie's and David's case. With all the federal cuts and their caseloads being so large, they usually go for the quick win. Lou did not like seeing his friend so uptight. He knew how badly he wanted this. Lou called Molly and asked her opinion. Molly had a good sense about these things. She was excited they bought the Morgan place and moving closer. It was great that he would be working part-time with Lou. She and his wife got along very well. As for telling Ray, she felt Lou should. They hung up, and Lou decided to tell him. When they arrived at the lockup, it was close to noon. Rivera's attorney was still there. No word was mentioned about a deal. Lou could see that Ray was at his wit's end.

Lou said, "Hey buddy, let's take a walk outside and discuss this." When they went outside, they both lit a cigar, and Lou asked, "What's up? I've never seen you like this."

Ray replied, "I don't know. I don't want to look like an ass in front of this judge if Rivera doesn't turn."

Lou replied, "I understand, but this is a seasoned judge. He knows these things don't always come together."

Ray replied, "Still. Every feather in my cap makes me a better candidate for this promotion. I really need this Lou. My family needs it."

Lou said, "I wasn't going to tell you this, but Molly said I should. You never knew this. Your boss and I went to college together. We are good friends. His family has visited a few times over the years. He loves our golf course. Since I was in town, I called to say hi. He was telling me he bought a place outside of the town where I live. He asked me to handle the real estate end for him and work with the contractor he set up to get the place ready for when he moved in. He told me he was retiring soon. I was happy to hear this and asked him if would consider working a couple of days a week in the office after he was settled. I needed experienced attorneys. He thought that was a great idea. He was not looking forward to sitting around seven days a week. I am sorry, but I had to ask who might be replacing him. I asked him who was in line for his job. He told me, three people. However, they had already decided that you were going to be offered the position. Please, do not breathe a word that I told you this."

Ray replied, "I won't. Thanks for letting me know. I am not mad you asked. You know; we are friends as well."

Lou replied, "Yes we are, and that's what friends do." They finished their cigars, and Ray asked, "Maybe you can help me to get Rivera to turn. I'm fresh out of ideas."

Lou, noticing that after hearing this news, Ray was much more relaxed. Lou did not lie about the outcome, but he did bend the truth a little as to how they arrived at it. Lou said, "Let's go have a crack at Rivera."

They had lunch delivered and had a quick bite to eat. As they were finishing, Rivera's attorney came out and wanted to meet with Ray and Anthony. Lou tagged along. They sat in the conference room and wait for him to speak.

He said, "Gentleman, I seem to be at an impasse with my client. We have been discussing his option for hours. He will not budge. He wants full immunity and the witness protection program. He feels with the information he has that can clear up many things. It's the only option he will take."

Lou said, "Excuse me sir, but your client has no idea what the new evidence we uncovered is. Maybe if we all met and informed him, he might think differently."

Rivera's attorney asked, "Than you are willing to deal?"

Ray replied, "If you want us all to meet. I will present the evidence and his options. Know this, the witness protection program will never be on the table, and you will both find out why if we all get together."

Rivera's attorney said, "Give me a minute with my client." After a few minutes passed, Rivera's attorney said, "My client will listen to what you have to say." Rivera was brought into the room.

Ray had the ammunition. All he had to do is pull the trigger, and he would have the smoking gun. Ray said, "Maybe it's time for a wake-up call. Let me fill you in on some things you do not know. First, we have the identity of the witness you bribed. Do you want to risk the fact that she will not roll over on you to avoid five years in prison for committing perjury? Second, we now have conclusive DNA evidence that your DNA was found in the trunk of David's car. I will prove you rented the white van. I will also prove how you obtained his credit card information. With this new evidence, and what your attorney has heard in court so far, I can prove without a doubt, this was the premeditated murder of an FBI agent. I will easily get the death penalty. As far as the witness protection program, forget it. You will never see it. For the government, this is a win, win situation. The only one who loses is you. However, I am interested in clearing up any other cases. I will offer one deal only. If you refuse it, you can appeal as much as you like, but the result will be a needle in your arm."

Rivera's attorney asked, "What is your offer?"

Ray said, "In return for his cooperation, and if it leads to arrests and convictions, I will take the death penalty off the table. Your client will receive a sentence of 150 years in prison. He will die there. I will also arrange to have him placed in a medium versus a maximum-security facility. He will be able to have visitors and conjugal visits. He will never be eligible for parole. That is the deal, the only deal. Talk about and let me know your decision within an hour. We do not have much time to put this together before the court convenes tomorrow. Once we step into that courtroom, there is no changing your mind. This is a one-time offer only. I suggest you take the time and consider this carefully. The clock is ticking"

Everyone but Rivera and his attorney got up and left the room. Rivera still was not happy with this. He felt he could easily be killed in prison. His attorney was now starting to get aggravated and said, "Are you stupid? Think. The reason he is putting you in a medium-security facility is so you will not be with the type of prisoners who would do that. Is there always a risk, of course? However, this is a much better option. The decision is yours. What I can tell you is this. With all the evidence, I cannot get you off, or even get your sentence reduced. What do you want to do?"

Rivera sat there for some time thinking. Even he realized he had no other choice. About forty-five minutes after everyone left the room, he said, "Make the deal." However, there is one stipulation. I am guaranteed to have a private cell."

Rivera's attorney called everyone back into the room. He addressed Ray and said, "My client will accept the deal with one stipulation."

Ray replied, "I already said that was the deal and started to get up."

Rivera's attorney said, "Hold on. At least hear what it is. I believe it is reasonable, or I would have never called you back." Lou leaned over to Ray and said, "Let's hear it."

Ray replied, "Okay, what is it?"

"My client will agree to all the terms of your offer providing he is guaranteed to always have a private cell. He doesn't want to spend the rest of his life having to sleep with one eye open."

Lou looked at Ray and gave him a nod expressing he should accept it. Ray said, "I had the agreement drawn to save time, and will have my clerk add this to it. When I return, we will go over it, get it signed, and notarized." Everyone agreed. Ray and Lou left the room.

Ray was still upset. Max was his friend. He wanted to see Rivera fry. However, being the good attorney that he was, he also knew Max would have wanted it this way to get many other cases solved, and others arrested. It was a huge win. The agreement was completed. When they met, everyone signed it, and it was notarized. Ray informed his boss. His boss gave Ray a teaser and said, "My office is scheduled to be painted next week. Is there a specific color you like because it will be yours soon?"

Ray thanked him and said, "No sir. The present color is fine."

He was thrilled. Lou and Ray went to see David and give him the news.

Russell's wife came into town to be in court tomorrow. When everyone was together, Ray and Lou told them the news. Once David was released, they would have a celebration dinner. Molly and Allie were grateful to everyone. They were now convinced David would be coming home. Tonight's dinner was Ray's treat.

CHAPTER 12

IS IT EVER REALLY OVER?

The time came. It was Friday morning. Ray, Anthony, Mike, and Lou had a meeting with the judge at nine o'clock to discuss these new findings and see how to proceed. When they met, they went over everything with the judge.

The judge said, "I will approve this plea bargain and have the charges dropped against David. However, no one has told me how you plan to get me what I asked for."

Mike said, "Your honor, will be my surprise. Let me get her back on the stand to complete my cross.

The judge said, "It's your show counselor."

Court started at ten sharp. The judge asked both sides if they had enough time to review the evidence, and ready to proceed. Both attorneys replied yes. The defense calls Ms. Angelina to the stand to complete their cross-examination. The judge informed her she was still under oath. Mike politely hammered her. He showed her the photos and all the evidence he had proving she was not who she claimed to be. She was panicking. She asked the judge if she could make a deal. The judge asked the clerk to repeat back everything regarding her testimony two days ago. The clerk read the complete transcript.

He sat back; he looked at her, and explained, "I do not have to, nor am I inclined to make a deal with you or any witness madam. The new evidence presented is so compelling; we have no need, nor a desire to make a deal. I am holding you in contempt of court and charging you will perjury. Madam, the reason I explained the definition to you was so there could be no misunderstanding as to whether you understood it or not. Marshals, please take the witness away."

Mike asked, "If there are no objections from the prosecution, and in light of the new evidence found and presented over the past two days, we have a signed plea bargain which your honor has seen. I request at this time that all charges against my client be dropped, and all references to this case are stricken from his record."

The judge asked the prosecution," Does the government have any objections?"

Anthony replied, "No your honor."

The judge explained, "I would like to thank the jury for their time and patience, and apologize they have been taken away from their families. However, we are here to find out the truth. That is the only way justice can be done. Without your cooperation and the cooperation of all the attorneys, we cannot reach that goal. Mr. Romano, please stand." David and his attorneys stood up. "This court orders that the charges in the matter of the government versus David Romano are now dropped. All reference to this matter is to be removed from Mr. Romano's record. Mr. Romano, congratulations."

David replied, "Thank you your honor."

The judge added, "Before I close this case and dismiss the jury, I would like to thank everyone involved for their time, and a job well done. Case dismissed." The gavel was struck, and this was now history. David was a free man.

David thanked everyone. Molly and Allie rushed to him and gave him a hug and a kiss, even Lou. No one ever doubted that David did not commit this crime, but remembering Allie's case, sometimes justice does not prevail. Everyone went to lunch before starting home. Lou informed everyone he would be planning a party soon, and to watch for the invitation. With the information Ray would receive from Rivera, it would clear up many cold cases, and really put the final nail in Vincent's coffin. He had days of interrogations ahead of him. Rivera and Vincent would be his last two cases before his promotion. If they were not completed before that, those cases were rock solid. Those and the other cold cases could be handled by the less senior attorneys. This was an example of excellent collaboration by all, in the name of justice and truth. This would form new bonds for everyone involved as they moved forward. David would be working with all these individuals many times again in the future. David finally had the opportunity to speak with Paulie. David was devastated by what happened to him. Lou's company limo was a stretch limo. Everyone was able to ride back together. Charlie, Lou's driver, was always thinking. He had flowers, champagne, as well as sandwiches in the back for the ride home. It might be a long ride due to Friday afternoon traffic.

Allie was telling David about the two people who came asking about her that one day. He told her she should not worry. They were probably reporters looking for a story. In Allie and David's life, nothing ever was as it appeared. Could that be true? On the way back, Allie and Molly discussed asked Lou and David to join them in Paris and make it an extended four or five-day get-a-way. The girls were surprised when they agreed. Everyone except for Lou and David fell asleep on the ride home. It was stressful past few days. It finally caught up to them. Lou and David discussed all the little details they each knew. David thanked Lou for agreeing to the recess for the extra two days. It was the right thing to do.

"Dad, I knew mom would be upset, but I relied on you to make the right choice. You did. Thank you."

Lou replied, "Don't be so quick to thank me. At first, I wanted to say no. Sometimes you forget that I am your father first. Those emotions run deep."

"I know they do. I am not only your son and you my father; we are also best friends. However, I know you Dad. You always do the right thing when you need to, no matter what. I am learning. I love you."

Lou replied, "I love you as well. Never forget that."

When they finally got home, David could not wait to see the baby. David and Lou thanked the housekeeper for staying there those few days, and Lou gave her a handsome tip. The bay was asleep, and he did not care. He woke him up. As soon as baby Louis saw him, his eyes lit up, and he smiled and started laughing.

Allie said with a chuckle, "Now you've done it. We'll never get him back to bed, and I had such plans for us tonight." Everyone was excited because, on Monday, Allie would find out if they were having a boy or a girl.

Before the housekeeper left, she walked over to Allie and said, "That gentleman came back the following day. Miss Allie, I was not going to tell him anything. This time he left his card and asked you to call him." Allie looked at the card. It was from someone named Stewart Cummings, a Private Investigator. Allie showed Lou and David the card.

Lou said, "Leave it with me. I'll handle it. Lou knew him from his days of doing his internship. He was in the PI game for years. He was a retired police officer that had to retire under disability when he was shot in the line of duty. It left him with a bad leg. He could no longer work as a police officer, and he did not want a desk job. He had a good disability pension and started this business. The baby went back to sleep. Everyone had coffee and relaxed. Allie was clinging to David as if she would never see him again.

Molly finally said, "Babe, let's go to bed before these two rip each other's clothes off on their couch."

It was not that late, but everyone was feeling frisky and probably needed to bond. Molly and Lou went back to their house, and Allie said, "Just wait here until I call you."

David sat in his chair. Looking around the room realizing just how much he missed being home. The town had a welcome home party planned for Saturday night in the church hall and had one of the local bands playing. He thought that would be fun. During the day tomorrow, he and Lou would go to the office and catch up, and the girls would be at the shop. Julie, the store manager, had been running things while Allie and Molly were away. They were looking forward to getting back to work. Actually, everyone was just looking forward to getting things back to normal. David was starting to doze off when he heard Allie call out to him to come in. As he walked down the hallway, he could smell her perfume. When he entered the room, there were candles lit, two glasses of wine poured, and Allie was lying on the bed wearing this cute outfit she bought when she and Molly went shopping yesterday.

David said, "Give me a minute to take a quick shower."

Allie replied, "Your minute is up. Come to bed."

David got undressed and got into bed with Allie. For two hours, they explored each other in every way possible. Their bodies were intertwined. They were as one; one being, one heart, one mind, and one soul. The passion they shared was deep and intense. There was not one part of each other, mentally, emotionally, or physically, that they did not love about one another. Two people from two different worlds, different pasts, never thinking they could ever find or want this type of life, found it in each other. They would be in love forever. No matter what life threw at them, they would always have each other.

When they were relaxing, Allie said to David, "We have been through more in the time we have been together than most go through in their entire life."

"There is something about us. I don't know if it relates to our past, or it's our personalities. Somehow I don't think this will be the last thing we are dragged into."

Allie replied, "Somehow I think you're right. We are a family. Together we can beat anything."

They both fell asleep.

*****

Saturday morning arrived. It was a beautiful day in New England. The leaves were just starting to look as if they would be turning colors soon. The fall was the most beautiful time of the year in

New England. It was not too hot, and not too cold. The colors were amazing. The girls headed to the shop in one car, and Lou and David to the office in another. When Lou and David got to the office, Lou sat down to call the private investigator. David sat with him. When he and Stewart connected, it was like two old friends who had not seen each other for years. He introduced David to Steward and explained how he was now a partner in the firm. Steward told him he had been following the case and was glad it all had been straightened out.

Steward said, "Lou, that brings to me to why I stopped at your house."

Lou replied, "Okay, what's going on?"

Steward said, "I was hired by Sarah Thomas, formerly Sarah Green, to find her daughter Allie. It had been nearly fifteen years since they spoke, and she wanted to make things right. She had heard about Allie from her case since it made national headlines, and now her clothing line."

David interjected and said, "Stop right there. Allie is my wife. We have spoken many times about her mother and offered many times to try to find her. Allie is dead set against that. She has no use for her mother and does not want to see her. What happened, did Brad finally leave her, and now she needs money?"

Steward said, "I can respect that David, but actually no. Brad passed away. She could not look for Allie when he was alive. Before he died, he confessed to all the things he had done to Allie. Sarah was devastated. He left her with a nice life insurance policy. She didn't need money. She wanted her daughter."

David said, "Stew, do not tell her that you found Allie."

Steward responded, "She already knows and stopped by the house. I told her that was the wrong thing to do. She should have never done that. She asked me to handle this for her. Dave, I understand how protective you are towards your wife. I would probably be the same way. However, don't you think that Allie has the right to know? Then she can make her own decisions?"

Lou looked and David with a look that meant Steward was right. David replied, "I'm sorry. I know you are right. However, Allie has been through so much. I do not know if this is the right time. Let me give it some thought. Tell her mother you spoke to us, and we will get back to you. Please let her know that if she comes back to the house before we give our approval, I will have her arrested. I want Allie to be aware of this first. No surprises."

Steward thanked them and agreed. However, he could only relay a message. He could not control what Sarah might do. That would be her choice. That night was the party. David did not want to spoil this time for Allie. Tomorrow would be as good a time as any to tell Allie. Everyone went to the party and had a wonderful time. The food was great, the company was great, and the music was fantastic. Everyone danced and had a great time. After the party, Lou told Molly about Allie's mother.

Molly was completely against it saying, "Babe, how much do you think one woman can take?"

Lou understood, but he explained that if they kept this from her, and she found out, how would she feel? He didn't say this to Molly, but he also felt Molly was afraid she might lose Allie. She looked upon her as a daughter, and Allie looked at Molly as her mother. He knew Molly would not want to lose that. As much as Molly was against it, she knew she should agree. Allie would have to make her own choices. They decided to tell Allie after church in the morning.

In the morning, they went to church. Allie must have eaten something that did not agree with her, and she got violently sick. She was throwing up and had diarrhea. They took her home and gave her some medicine. She was relaxing on the couch and fell asleep. When she awoke, she felt drawn out. She was probably slightly dehydrated. She took in some fluids and started to feel better. Molly, Lou, and David decided that this was not the time to tell her. Actually, they did not want to tell her before their Paris trip. It had been almost fifteen years, what would another seven days matter? Monday came, and off they went to the doctor with Allie. She was far enough along to determine the sex of the baby. It was a GIRL! Everyone was so excited, especially Molly. She was praying for a granddaughter.

At dinner that night, Allie said, "I have an announcement to make." Everyone got quiet. "David and I talked about this. Mom, dad, you are more of mother and father to me than my own parents were, and also great friends. We are a family in every sense. David and I have decided to name the baby Jessica."

Molly burst out crying. They were tears of surprise and joy. She hugged Allie so hard; Allie had to let her know to loosen up a bit. Lou also had tears rolling down his face. He knew this meant the world to Molly and him as well. Allie had just made Lou and Molly the happiest grandparents in the world.

Allie went on to say, "We weren't sure if this would upset you losing Jessica the way you did. However, we knew this was something we wanted to do."

Molly said, "Upset us, NEVER! You could not have honored us in any better way."

At that moment, Lou's phone rang. It was Ray. He said, "Lou, I wanted you to know, and I already notified Jeff, the Chief of Police. While transferring Rivera, he escaped. We have a tri-state manhunt out for him. We will catch him, but I just wanted you to know."

He had a concerned look on his face. Molly asked, "Babe, what is it?"

Lou stated, "It was Ray. Rivera escaped. Don't worry, they will catch him."

That news was upsetting. At that exact moment, the doorbell rang. Everyone knew Rivera could not have gotten there already, and would certainly not ring the doorbell. Would he even try? Allie was by the door and said, "I'll get it."

When Allie opened the door, a woman was standing there. Allie said, "Can I help you?"

The woman replied, "Allie. I would know you anywhere. Don't you recognize me? I'm Sarah, your mother." Allie just stood there in shock.

- The End -

**Watch for the final book in the three book murder mystery series
Life Through A Mirror, "When Murder Calls." Coming May 2019.
Find out how Allie's mother, Rivera, and these other cases cause
Allie, David, and the family, to be dragged into another murder.**

CREDITS

Book cover design - Jodilocks Cover Designs

Printed in the United States
By Bookmasters